An Indep...

The Tale of Betsy Dowdy and Black Bess

by Donna Campbell Smith

First Edition

Legends of the Carolinas Series

Coastal Carolina Press
Wilmington, NC

An Independent Spirit:
The Tale of Betsy Dowdy and Black Bess
Donna Campbell Smith

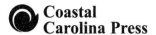

Coastal
Carolina Press

www.coastalcarolinapress.org

First Edition

An Independent Spirit:
The Tale of Betsy Dowdy and Black Bess
is a publication in Coastal Carolina Press's
Legends of the Carolinas Series.

Cover and book design by Robert Bunch, Intrepid Media
Cover illustration and interior illustrations by Debi Davis
Map by Donna Campbell Smith

Printed in Canada

Applied for Library of Congress Cataloging-in-Publication Data

ISBN 1-928556-35-3

10 9 8 7 6 5 4 3 2 1

This book is dedicated to the memory of my sister, Claudia Campbell Huband.

Books in the
Legends of the Carolinas Series

Pale As the Moon

An Independent Spirit

Coastal Carolina Press's *Legends of the Carolinas Series*
is devoted to adventure-filled historical novels for young adults.

Acknowledgements

Without the support and encouragement of family and friends I would never have gotten past saying, "Someday, I want to write a book."

I thank my family: Julia, Deborah, Michael, Camille, and Jessica, who were required to listen to me talk endlessly about "my book." A special thanks goes to my daughter, Dineane, for her honest proofing.

The members of Bottom Line Writers' Group I thank for listening and critiquing. Kathy and Lisa, for going the extra mile, thank you. My fellow writers at www.writersbbs.com, I appreciate your encouragement, advice, and honest critiques.

To my best friends—Mary Jane Watson, who said it was okay for me to be a little bit proud, Angela Natho for her genuine good wishes, and Dae Chapin for all the lunches where she listened to me go on and on.

Emily Colin, my editor, and all of the staff at Coastal Carolina Press, you have put up with my uncertainties and made it happen—twice. Thank you. I am especially grateful to Debi Davis, whose art I have long appreciated.

And to my Lord, whose presence I acknowledge.

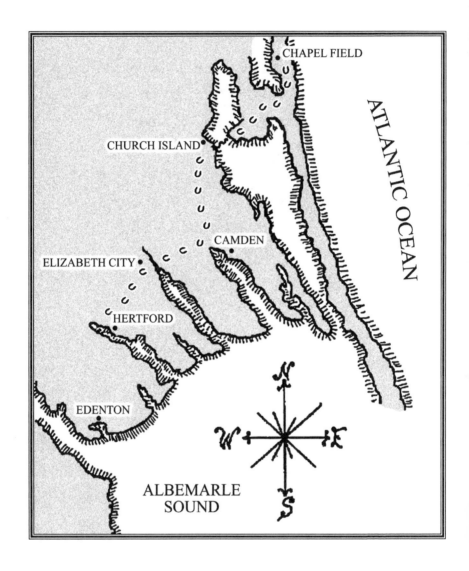

CHAPEL FIELD

CHURCH ISLAND

CAMDEN

ELIZABETH CITY

HERTFORD

EDENTON

ATLANTIC OCEAN

ALBEMARLE
SOUND

Chapter One

November 1774

We stood on the top of Penny's Hill, my pony and I. I could see the back side of Currituck Island and across the sound all the way to the mainland. To the east the ocean stretched until it disappeared into the sky. On the far side of the ocean I imagined I could see the green hills of Ireland, home of my ancestors.

At the bottom of the dunes, on the sound side, the geese were flying in to settle down for the night. They came here every year to spend the winter. There were so many of them, they blacked out the sun like a thundercloud. That's where Currituck got its name; it is Indian for 'land of many geese.'

Below us was the wild pony herd. Black

Bess's mama belonged to that herd. The horses grazed on the tough grass that grew in a little hammock between the sand dunes. From our vantage point on top of the dune Bess could see her relatives, and whinnied a greeting to them. I felt her body vibrate under me.

"Tougher'n nails," Grandpa said of the ponies, "been on these islands for about two hundred years. The sea makes anything tough that can survive it."

I'd lived on this island all my life, watching and loving these horses. They were not actually two hundred years old, of course. Their ancestors had come over on ships with Spanish explorers two hundred years ago. Some people say the horses swam ashore when the explorers' boats wrecked off the coast, or that they were brought here when the explorers came this way looking for gold and other riches.

Grandpa's version of the story was that the Spanish explorers did not find what they were looking for. The Indians ran them off so fast, they left their horses and livestock behind.

"Hightailed it for Florida and left these horses to fend for themselves. And fend for themselves they did," Grandpa said. He loved the wild ponies as much as I.

He helped me tame Black Bess. I saw her for the first time when she was only a few days old. Black as the ace of spades, she was. And always so full of herself, bucking and frolicking around her mama, who just ignored her antics and went on grazing.

When I told Grandpa about her, he couldn't wait to have a look-see. He stopped right in the middle of mending nets and followed me up the beach.

The filly ran a circle around the little dune

where her mama stood grazing, and then she peeked out from behind. All of a sudden, she ran back hard as she could and play-kicked at her mama. Her mama ignored her, and just kept on munching grass.

"Just like you," Grandpa laughed, "plumb full of herself."

We were best friends from the start. Grandpa and I started getting her used to us right away. We brought her treats, like kernels of corn and carrots. Bess soon let me pet and brush her. By the time she was a two-year-old, I could do anything with her. My beautiful, black pony didn't mind a bit the first time I rode her.

After Grandpa died, Bess helped fill the hole left in my heart. He was old and Mother said he had lived a good life. But I missed him, missed him a lot.

Grandpa had been a sailor, the captain of a

whaling ship. He was from Ireland, but he'd been all around the world and never found a place finer than Currituck Banks, where he stayed and raised his family.

After Grandpa retired from sailing, he worked as a fisherman. He used to take me out on his skiff to run the nets. I helped sort the fish and then we'd carry them over to the mainland to sell.

Grandpa once told me that being out on the sea was the closest anyone could get to God this side of heaven. I know now what he meant. It's so quiet and peaceful there. I wasn't allowed to take the boat out by myself, but even on shore I felt like Grandpa was right by my side. If I listened real carefully I could still hear him talk to me.

I slipped off Bess and sat down in the sand. The sky was beginning to turn a soft pink. A few geese squabbled over territory, honking and flapping their wings at each other. Behind me, on the ocean side, I could hear the rhythmic pounding of the surf.

Bess dropped her head to nibble at some sea oats. She made the grass scritch as she pulled at it with her teeth. Wrapping my arms around my knees, I watched the seagulls swoop down into the waves and come back up with their dinner. I was sure that these islands were the most wonderful place in all the world.

Feeling peaceful but lonely, I took a long, deep breath of the ocean air. The sun was setting and sinking slowly into the sound. A brilliant gold edged the clouds, like the frame around the painting of Grandpa Dowdy that hung in our dining room. A few minutes later the sky got pinker with splashes of red and orange.

"Red at night, sailor's delight," I heard Grandpa say. He said that when there was a pretty sunset, and he was always right. I thought of the stories about his adventures at sea and his tales about ghosts and Indian legends. And all the things he taught me, like how to fish and ride and sail and row a canoe. He didn't treat me like a girl; he said I could do anything I put my mind to.

"What you can do doesn't have anything to do with being a girl or a boy or strong or weak. It's got to do with how bad you want to do it, and how hard you are willing to try," he'd said.

It started breezing up. I shivered and pulled my cloak tighter around my shoulders. The surf and the rattling of the sea oats tempted me to linger, but I knew my parents would worry about me if I stayed out after dark.

Family and friends were coming the next day for our annual oyster roast. Since this was Mother's chance to put on a Banker-style to-do, it always became a huge feast. Our neighbor, Mr. Jarvis, would bring his fiddle and we would dance afterwards. Mother always worried about the weather, because our house was not big enough to hold all the people we were expecting.

"Come on girl, we better go home before Father comes looking for us," I said to Bess.

I gathered the bottom of my skirt and tucked the hem into my waistband, so it looked like I was wearing big puffy britches. Then I grabbed Bess's mane with my left hand, set my right hand on her withers and vaulted onto her back. She turned her head, looked at me in reproach for interrupting her snack, and then started down the sand dune toward home. The beach spread before us, awash in crimson, as the last of the sun slowly sank into Currituck Sound.

By the time I got home it was almost dark. The scrunch-scrunch of Bess's hooves on the oyster shell path that led up to the house announced our return.

Chapel Field was the name Grandpa gave our home on Currituck Banks. Our two-story house was built of strong cypress wood and the roof of cedar shingles, weathered to a silvery gray. Grandpa had built the house forty years before, and a fine job he'd done. The house survived many a nor'easter and hurricane without a bit of damage. It had two rooms downstairs separated by a hallway in the middle. On the hottest summer days, we opened the back and front doors at either end of the hall and let the air breeze through. A wide porch wrapped around the front and sides of the house. It helped shade out the sun and made a fine place to sit and shell peas, sew, or just daydream. Upstairs was the same, with tall windows instead of doors. All of the windows were tall to let in the breeze. Shutters protected the panes from breaking whenever there was a storm.

"Well, it's about time my wandering girl came home," Father said as he opened the front door, letting the warm glow of lamplight pour onto the porch.

I could see him smiling at me. Father had Grandpa's smile. He was tall and thin like Grandpa, too, but still had a head full of sun-bleached hair. Grandpa had had a bald spot fringed with a wreath of gray.

"I'm sorry to be late. I was watching the ponies, and the sunset. It's going to be a pretty day for tomorrow's oyster roast. You know what Grandpa always said, 'Red at night, sailors delight, red in the morning, sailors take warning.'"

Father walked out onto the porch. He took a deep breath of the salty air and stretched. Then he leaned against the post and watched me. "You are right, Betsy," he agreed, "it was a beautiful sunset. I am sure your mother will be relieved about the weather."

Bess stood quietly while I brushed her down. I reached for my wooden groom's box, put the brush away, and pulled out an ear of dried corn. I always had a treat tucked into my box to thank Bess for the ride.

"There you go. Off with you now." I handed my pony the corn and patted her on the rump. Then I joined Father on the porch. He smiled at me and we watched Bess trot away, disappearing into the weathered myrtle bushes and across the dunes to join the herd.

From the Diary of Rebecca Dowdy
November 28, 1774

My Betsy is a beautiful young lady, but it was hard to see that tonight. When she came in the house, well after dark, she smelled like a horse, her auburn hair was wind-tangled, and she had her skirt pulled up between her long legs with the hem tucked into her waistband.

She has no idea how much it frightens me for her to be wandering out on the beach and among the dunes riding that wild pony. Anything could happen. I know she explores the forest as well. There are wild beasts in that forest. But the fauna is not my only concern. These Outer Banks are refuge to all sorts of misfits that might prey upon a young and beautiful girl.

It especially distresses me for her to be out past dark. And though I am constant in reprimanding her for it, she continues to lose track of the time. I do not understand why she cannot see well enough that the sun is setting; I think she just disregards my warnings.

I chastised her for her tardiness. She expressed sincere regret and retired to her room, closing the door.

That closed door symbolizes our relationship, for it is not only the door to her bedchamber that shuts me out, it is the door to her spirit.

Josiah says I am too hard on her and that I should just give her time to grow up. He says she should be allowed to enjoy her youth while she can, that Betsy will come to know the reality of life soon enough. I am not sure I agree with him. Betsy is no longer a child; she is fourteen years old. It is time she learned to behave like a young lady and not some wild wood nymph. How else will she ever find a suitable husband? I want her to enjoy a good life, without toil and pain. How can that be unless she marries well?

No, wild ponies cannot give my Betsy a happy life. That is all I want for her—happiness.

Chapter Two

The next morning I woke up to the sound of the geese honking and squawking. After I made my bed I wasted no time getting dressed. Mother would find plenty for me to do, getting ready for our guests. I looked out the window and saw that my weather prediction had been correct. The sky was clear, and the sound was slick calm. On my way to feed the animals, I ran down the stairs to the dining room, where Mother was setting the table for breakfast.

"Good morning, Mother."

Mother nodded without giving me a word. She didn't think it was proper for me to care for the livestock, but I so loved the animals that long ago Grandpa convinced her to let me.

"We aren't planters like your kin over on the

mainland, with slaves to do our dirty work," he'd said. "Betsy knows how to pull her weight, and I, for one, am very proud of her."

We were Quakers and did not believe in owning slaves. Grandpa thought it was a sin that Aunt Frances and Uncle John, my mother's sister and brother-in-law, used slave labor on their plantation.

We did have outside help, though. Annie was the woman my father hired to cook and help Mother out with the house. She and her husband, Mr. O'Reilly, were getting on in years. They lived in a little house on the sound about a mile south of Chapel Field. All their children were grown.

Mr. O'Reilly worked with Father on the fishing boat. I loved to listen to the old man tell stories of the days when pirates used to hide in the sounds and inlets of the banks. His favorite one was about the time his Pa had the pirate Blackbeard to dinner. Mr. O'Reilly claimed that the gold coin he wore around his neck had been given to him by the infamous pirate. I wasn't sure that I believed the story, but I loved to hear him tell it.

Wonderful odors were wafting out from the kitchen. The kitchen was built separate from the main part of the house because cooking heated up the house so bad in the summer. Also, if Annie caught it afire, it wouldn't burn the whole house down.

I jumped over the three steps and through the door. Annie handed me a pail of scraps for the pigs.

"Mm, your cooking smells so good, Annie. I can taste it already."

Annie just nodded. She never talked much, but she was without a doubt the best cook in all of Carolina.

I could already taste the baked ham encrusted with sugar. We always had a ham when kin were coming. I knew there'd be candied yams, fodder beans, collard greens, and creamed potatoes, not to mention steamed shrimp and fish chowder. My favorite of all was the fried cornbread. Annie dropped spoonfuls of batter into boiling hot lard. In a few seconds they puffed up and turned golden brown. They were so delicious. And the desserts—sweet potato pie, apple pie, pound cake with straw-berry preserves and whipped cream—I groaned just thinking about them. Folks used to say don't eat sweets with oysters, but I never minded that rule.

Mixing dried corn into the bucket of leftovers

25

and pouring the slop into a wooden trough, I called, "Piiigeees! Piigees! Piggy, piggy, piggy!" Soon the whole herd of swine came running out of the rushes and into the feed pen. The pigs snorted and shoved, each trying to be first to breakfast. They were descendants of livestock brought to the coast by early explorers, too. We allowed them to run free in the marshes. Every morning, we called them in and fed them a little corn and scraps, just so we could catch them when need be. After Christmas we would select some to pen up and fatten out on corn until spring. The corn made the meat taste better, took away the wild flavor. Father smoked the pork, which provided ham and bacon all year.

My other chores were feeding the chickens, gathering eggs, and milking Moonbeam, our cow. Grandpa was the one who taught me to milk

Moonbeam. She was flighty; you had to do it just right or she'd hold back her milk. He taught me to warm my hands first on a cold morning and to squeeze her teats gently from top to bottom. I sang to her if she was particularly nervous.

"Thank you, Miss Betsy," Annie said when I came back inside. She held the door open and took the pail of milk and basket of eggs. Annie always thanked me for helping her with the chores.

I hurried to the main house where Mother waited impatiently.

"Your father is at the table. Clean off the barn-yard smell and have some breakfast." Mother's sense of smell was very acute. She always complained that I smelled like the livestock or horses or something disagreeable.

I washed my hands at the bowl in the hall and

joined Father in the dining room. "Not many eggs," I said. "Soon there won't be any at all with winter coming on."

"Yes, I know. We'll just have to enjoy them while we can, dear," Mother said in a tone that indicated she didn't care to talk about the eggs or think about where they came from. I changed the subject to the day's festivities.

Our neighbor Mr. Jarvis was first to arrive for the oyster roast. He brought a wagon pulled by his favorite Banker pony, Juney Bug, a chestnut mare with a blazed face. Heaped in a big pile on the wagon were fresh oysters and two-bushel baskets of shrimp. Father and Mr. Jarvis set about laying the wood in an outdoor fireplace.

My grandpa built that fireplace out of ballast stones brought to the port in Elizabeth City in ships from England. The stones were unloaded and replaced with tobacco, pine tar and other things that we in the colonies sent back to the mother country. Almost everyone in northeast North Carolina had some of these rocks, since in our area there were no rocks, just sand and dirt. They were used for everything from chimneys to foundations for our houses.

By the time the fire burnt down to red-hot coals, our other guests had arrived. The men put the oysters in big flat iron pans and set them on the fire. They covered the oysters with wet burlap bags. Soon steam rose and started to cook the oysters. When they were done cooking, we'd dump them out onto long tables in the back yard, open them with a special knife, and eat them right out of the shells. Some of the oyster shells always had tiny, succulent pink crabs hiding in them. Most of the girls did not care for the thought of eating a crab, legs and all, but I found them very tasty.

Like at every oyster roast we've ever had, the men gathered around the fire and talked all day. They made a big to-do out of getting the fire just right. The women usually stayed in the house or sat in chairs out on the front porch. They didn't often talk about anything of interest to me. I preferred listening to the men.

That was how I'd gotten into my first horse race a few years ago. Isaac Druman, the son of Earl Druman from Edenton, was bragging about his fancy stallion he'd had shipped over from London. The Drumans were rich planters, friends of Aunt Frances and Uncle Jonathan. Isaac bragged that there wasn't a horse in all the colonies that could beat Diablo.

Then Grandpa spoke up. "I wouldn't be too sure about that. You ought to see Betsy's little Banker flying down the beach!"

I just about choked on the raw oyster I'd put in my mouth. We always sampled a few raw while we were waiting for the fire to get right.

Isaac laughed. That made my cheeks red. He was so arrogant. All he really wanted was for everyone to know how rich he was, that he could import a racehorse from England. But I didn't say anything. Mother was always chastising me for being unladylike, so I knew I wasn't supposed to get into an argument, especially with one of our guests.

I will never forget what happened next for as long as I live. Grandpa set the whole thing up without telling Mother or Father. In fact, he didn't even tell me until the morning before the race. I was milking Moonbeam and Grandpa was feeding the chickens when he told me about it. It's a wonder Moonbeam didn't kick me to kingdom come, I squeezed her teat so hard.

The next day, we got up at the break of dawn and walked down to the boat dock. I sat in the boat with Grandpa and held onto Bess's lead rope while she swam alongside. The water was shallow most of the way across the Currituck, but all the same, Bess could swim like a goose.

By the time we reached shore a crowd was waiting for us.

"What are all of these people doing here?"

"They're here to see you beat that fancy English horse," Grandpa said. I could see that Grandpa was really expecting me to win that race.

He was grinning from ear to ear.

To tell the truth I was having my doubts. My Black Bess had just swum across the sound; I thought she was bound to be tired.

Grandpa tied the boat, and I hopped onto my pony's back. I didn't have a saddle. I used the halter and rope for a bridle.

"Hey, Betsy!" "Atta girl, Betsy!" I heard shouts from the crowd.

The race was a quarter-mile down a sandy cart track. Two young boys stretched a rope across the road marking the finish. I rode to the starting line, next to Isaac and his English stallion. The stallion was dancing and prancing, on his hind legs a goodly part of the time, anxious to run. He was already in a lather.

Bess seemed calm, but alert. The only races

we had ever run were with the seagulls on the beach, but I knew Bess was fast, and more important, running in the sand had put her in top condition. Even after swimming the sound, her breathing was unlabored. I was feeling more confident. She could run a quarter-mile and never care.

Isaac looked down his aristocratic nose and sneered at me sitting bareback on my Banker pony. Before I had time enough to get mad, a man hollered, "Get ready, get set, go!" and fired a pistol.

I squeezed my legs, leaned forward, and shouted to Bess, "Run, girl, run!"

Bess understood perfectly. When she felt my legs against her ribs she gathered her hind legs under herself and vaulted forward. Isaac's horse reared straight into the air, and by the time he was on all fours again, Bess and I were two lengths ahead of them.

"Run faster, girl," I urged. The sound of the stallion's hooves digging into the sandy path was getting closer.

Bess ran faster. I could feel her powerful muscles and the heat from her body through my own. A vision of Mother swooning over me showing my bare legs popped into my head. I pushed the thought away and concentrated on beating Isaac Druman's highfaluting horse.

Behind me, I heard Isaac smacking his horse's hindquarters with a crop. They were so close I could hear the stallion breathing.

Bess kept running and the finish rope got closer.

Suddenly I saw Diablo's head from the corner of my eye. He was gaining on us! On either side of the track, men were yelling, some jumping up and down. "Go, Betsy, go!" I heard them screaming.

"Come on man, are you going to let a girl on a Banker pony beat you?" I heard another say.

Isaac was alongside of us, still gaining.

I waited until we were about four horse lengths away from the finish line before I gave Bess some final words of encouragement. "Come on, Bess, run! Beat that smart aleck or we'll never hear the end of it. Beat him!" I squeezed my legs harder and held on tight.

Bess almost sprinted out from under me. Her ears flat and her neck stretched forward, she ran, her legs gathering under her and then reaching out in long smooth strides.

The next thing I heard was the people in the crowd screaming at the top of their voices, "She won! She won!"

Grandpa was jumping up and down, waving

his arms. Then he ran over and gave me a big hug, which made me fall off of Bess. If he had not still been hugging me I would have fallen out right in front of everyone, because my knees were like jelly.

Mother got so mad when she found out, she cried for a week. That is when she started talking about me going to stay with Aunt Frances in Edenton, so I could learn to behave like a lady.

Chapter Three

Mother believed it was unseemly for a young lady to be outside listening to the men talk while they cooked the oysters. Grandpa used to say, "Leave her be, Rebecca. She's having fun. I'll send her inside after a while."

This time I didn't have Grandpa to take up for me. I waited until Mother was distracted with her guests before I made my getaway.

About a dozen men had joined Father and Mr. Jarvis. They ranged in age from twelve-year-old Johnny, my first cousin, to old Mr. Sawyer from Church Island, who had to be ninety if he was a day. There were about thirty young'uns running around playing on the sand dunes and chasing geese.

The men's conversation centered mostly on

politics. There was some talk about the storm that had breezed through here last month and the run of bluefish that hit last week, and then they went back to the same boring subject.

"You hear tell about that meeting ole Daniel Earle had going down in Edenton?" I heard Uncle John say.

I had heard, and so had most everybody, I was sure. Rev. Earle from St. Paul's had gotten a group of townsfolk stirred up over taxes King George had put on the colonies. Said the cause of Boston was our cause, too. I wasn't that interested in what went on in Boston, or Edenton either for that matter.

"Well, last month Penelope Barker stirred up a fuss. She rallied the women in Edenton together for a meeting at Mrs. Elizabeth King's house. They wrote up a proclamation of their own. Says they won't drink another spot of tea or wear any clothes made in England until the Mother Country repeals the Stamp Act and stops taxing us for goods sold and bought."

"I bet she wouldn't be carrying on like that were it not for her husband, Thomas, still being stranded in the Mother Country," said a portly man as he popped another oyster in his mouth.

Some of the men laughed. I guessed they considered it unlikely the ladies could go long without their tea and fashionable dresses. It made little difference to me. We drank Indian tea made from native plants and herbs in Mother's garden. As for fashions, our clothes were made of Osnabrig, a homespun cloth. In fact, I didn't know of a thing we needed that we didn't have right here on the islands.

Not finding the conversation of interest, I

41

decided to check on the ponies. Before I could even get out of the back yard, up ran Johnny.

"Can I come with you?" he asked. I wanted to say no, but that would have been rude.

"I reckon. I'm just going to walk up the beach and see Bess."

"Can we ride? Have there been any ship-wrecks lately? Uncle John says you Banker people live off salvage that comes washing up on the beach after shipwrecks." Johnny took a quick breath and then went on, "And he says that pirates come up into the sound to hide, and you invite them in to dinner!"

"Don't be daft. There haven't been any pirates around here for years. You must have been listening to O'Reilly's stories." I walked faster, satisfied to hear Johnny huffing and puffing, trying to keep up with me in the soft sand.

He was all but right about the shipwrecks, though. Once Grandpa and I found a bunch of bananas washed up on the beach after a hurricane. I didn't have any idea what they were, but Grandpa knew. He knew everything, having traveled all over the world in his younger days. I'd never tasted anything like them before or since. If we'd had to live off salvage from shipwrecks, we'd have been in bad shape. No, we lived by hard work, which Johnny didn't know anything about. He lived the life of leisure, Uncle John being a planter and owning slaves who did all of the work.

"There they are," I said.

The little band of horses was standing in a grove of trees on the back side of a ridge of sand dunes. A white snowy egret was sitting right on the back of one of the horses. I whistled and Bess threw

43

her head up and looked at me. Then she came trotting our way. Her black coat shone so it looked almost blue, but her thick, silky mane was knotted and tangled from the wind.

"Do you still want to go for a ride?" I tucked up my skirt and hopped up on Bess's back.

"Don't you use a bridle or saddle?" Johnny looked worried.

"I don't need either. Come on, take my hand." I reached down and pulled his arm as he scrambled up behind me.

"How do you tell her which way to go without a bridle?"

"She just knows." I squeezed my legs and Bess started trotting.

"Slow down! Slow down!"

"For goodness's sake, I thought you wanted to

ride up the beach. Hold on, you'll be fine." I squeezed my legs and leaned forward, urging Bess into a full gallop.

Well, he held on all right. I thought he was going to squeeze the life right out of me. Away we went, seagulls laughing at Johnny wailing behind me. Before he fainted with fear, I slowed Bess down to a walk. All I had to do was shift my weight back a little, and she knew just what I wanted.

"See, I told you you'd be fine. You didn't fall off, did you?"

When I turned around to look at my cousin, his face was as white as a yard goose.

Chapter Four

I made Bess walk all the way back home. What a baby my cousin was.

We got back just as Father and Mr. Jarvis dumped the first pan of steamed oysters onto the table. I gave Bess an ear of corn, then turned her loose. Johnny brushed himself off before running around to the back yard. He didn't want horsehair on his new britches. Good thing he couldn't see himself from behind. I giggled because the spot of dirt and horsehair where he'd been sitting made it look like he'd wet his britches. Maybe he *had* wet his britches, he was so scared.

Even though we were eating outside, the dining tables were covered with white linen tablecloths and set with Mother's china and silver.

Father and Mr. Jarvis were shucking out oysters and putting them in little bowls for the ladies. The men stood around a table made of old boards, piled high with oysters, and ate as fast as they could scoop them out of their shells. Needless to say, the oyster table had no tablecloth.

"Betsy, here! I found a crab in this one," Mr. Jarvis called. He knew how I loved those little pink crabs. A melody of voices, spiked with laughter, floated across the yard while we ate oysters and threw the empty shells in a pile at the end of the table. The pile grew higher and higher as the afternoon wore on.

By sunset everyone had eaten their fill. I helped Annie clear the tables, and we lit smoky torches to keep away the skeeters. Had it not been for the ocean breeze, the torches wouldn't have been a bit of help. Even in October, if there was a landward breeze on a warm night, the skeeters could be so thick you couldn't take a breath without sucking one up your nose.

When it got dark the young'uns played mee-honkey. They hid among the dunes and rushes, calling out like geese to make it easier for whoever was "it" to find them. The goose call sounds like "meehonkey," which is how the game got its name.

Soon we moved indoors. Earlier in the day Mother, Annie, and I had moved all the furniture back and rolled up the carpet in the parlor to make room. Mr. Jarvis took out his fiddle and people started dancing. Those who were not dancing gathered about in the yard and on the front porch, where they could talk and listen to the fiddle-playing.

People were still discussing the ladies over in Edenton and their tea proclamation, and how up in Boston things were getting real bad. The farmers were upset about the taxes King George had levied on many of the products that were grown in America and shipped abroad. Things shipped in to us, like tea, we had to pay a tax for as well. Those of us that lived here on the islands weren't affected by the taxes much, since we didn't do a lot of farming. We grew enough to take care of ourselves, and didn't need very many things from the outside.

All that talk of politics was boring me to death. Slipping away from the party, I walked down the path to the boat dock. Grandpa's old skiff was tied up there. I stepped in and stretched out on my back in the bottom of the boat. Like a baby's cradle, the boat rocked back and forth in the water.

The sky was black as ink and dotted with millions of stars. Mr. Jarvis's fiddle music floated out to the sound and blended with the tunes played by the crickets in the marsh. I could feel Grandpa smiling down on me from heaven. Life was good here on Currituck Banks.

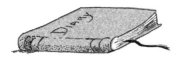

From the Diary of Rebecca Dowdy

November 29, 1774

I am tired to my bones. It was well past ten before all of our guests left. Of course Jonathan, Frances, and Johnny stayed the night.

It was a good party for such primitive conditions. I am thankful we had nice weather, with an ocean breeze. An ocean breeze blows the mosquitoes away, which is always a blessing.

It is disturbing to watch Betsy growing up here. She is as wild as those ponies she loves. Grandpa Dowdy encouraged her behavior from the time she could walk. He filled her head with stories about pirates and whaling and fighting Indians. As if the stories were not enough, he'd take her out fishing in that old skiff, and of course it was he that taught her to ride.

51

Well, he is gone now. We all miss him. Betsy suffered melancholy for a good while after his passing. She seems much better now. The horse has been a solace to her, and for that I am grateful.

Josiah is just like his father, taking up for Betsy all the time. He fails to see the importance of Betsy being schooled, and is resisting the whole idea of her going to stay with Frances. He keeps telling me to leave her be.

Betsy is a beautiful girl—or I might say, young woman. Her auburn hair glistens in the sun and her emerald eyes dance with fire. As much as I often worry about her safety, I can't help loving her spirit. That girl does not know what fear means. And she has a genuine gift with animals. She fell in love with that horse the first day she laid eyes on it.

Once she started riding I never knew where to

find her. She and her Banker pony roam all up and down these islands. Some days she comes home soaking wet.

"It was so hot, Mother, Bess and I thought we would go for a swim," is the answer she gives to my inquiries.

Tomorrow Frances, Betsy, and I are going to knit hats and socks to send the militia. Betsy will be more miserable than the wind, but she can sit still long enough to knit some woolen caps. It's just simple knitting, not as complicated as the stockings. I know I will be doing well if I can keep her here past noon.

Well, I am tired. It was a wonderful party, but so much work.

Chapter Five

Mother made me stay in all the next day knitting those caps for the militia. I knew the poor men up in Boston were freezing and they needed their heads warmed, but I hated the monotony of knitting. Johnny got to fish and play on the beach the whole time I was forced to stay indoors with my mother and Aunt Frances. We made right many hats, though.

I was delighted to be released from my drudgery after tea. We didn't normally have afternoon tea, except when there were guests. Of course it was an herbal from our own garden, not imported tea.

Mother was in her element, gossiping about this and that. Now, Aunt Frances could say a word, and she was not lost for words on that day.

"You heard about the meeting we had with

Penelope Barker? Why, that woman is a character. She's buried two husbands and is raising a passel of children. And with her husband stranded in England I don't see where she finds the time to concern herself with politics.

"Everything she said at the meeting made perfect sense. It is the least we can do to stand behind our menfolk and neighbors to the north, who are suffering so much hardship, to drink our own herbal teas and boycott all English products. Why, the Brits have closed Boston Harbor with the Intolerable Acts. And of course that's why poor Thomas Barker can't come home to his family."

Aunt Frances went on to tell all there was to tell and then some about the folks in Edenton: who was sweethearts, who'd had a new baby, and how old Sam Newton had made off with the Spruills's pig and, when he got found, spent a day in the stocks on the town square. I'd of liked to see that.

She told about the fancy Christmas ball that was being planned by the town's leading ladies. "You know you are all invited. Betsy will have so much fun," she said, like I wasn't even there in the same room. Mother gave me a hard look, so I didn't say a word or roll my eyes.

Fun? I could just see me at a ball in my homespuns. I couldn't abide how silly those Edenton girls were, giggling and whispering behind their fans. I'd been with Mother to visit Aunt Frances, and once Aunt Frances had us go with her to a picnic on the town square. I saw how those girls acted. All they could talk about was who was wearing the fanciest gown, and if a young man even looked their way, they practically fainted.

Aunt Frances must have read my mind about my homespun dresses, because she said, "Betsy, don't you worry a bit about what to wear. I have gowns to spare and Rose can make the alterations. Oh, it will be wonderful. You know there are plenty of eligible young men in Edenton. Once we get your hair fixed and find you some decent clothes, I am sure one of them will take an interest. Won't they, Rebecca?"

Mother smiled. "It sounds lovely, Frances."

As soon as Mother let me leave, I ran for the dunes to find Bess. Johnny called out to me, but I pretended I didn't hear him. I needed to get as far away from all of that talk as I could.

Bess must have wondered where I'd been all

day. She cantered up before I could call out to her. I sprung up on her back and off we went, galloping down the beach. Waves broke at Bess's hooves and splashed against my legs. Even though it was the last day of November, the air wasn't cold. Seagulls dived into the rolling sea and came back up with silvery fish in their beaks. The sky was blue with plump white clouds scattered across.

I pulled off my cap and unpinned my hair. The wind felt so good blowing through my hair as I rode. I thought, *this is what freedom feels like, the wind in your hair and the sun on your back and a trusted horse to ride.*

Those girls on the mainland didn't know what they were missing. They could knit hats, dance in their grand halls, write their proclamations, and have their tea parties, but they would never know what freedom really felt like. We, who lived on the Banks, who could look out our windows and watch the dolphins play in the surf, we who could fall asleep to the music of the ocean's song, we truly knew freedom.

Chapter Six

I rode Bess north, almost to the inlet. Then we crossed the dunes and rode into the thick growth of twisted, stunted live oaks. The ground was dense with tall grass and vines. I had to lay flat on Bess's back, my arms wrapped around her neck and my face buried in her mane so I didn't get tangled up in the low-hanging branches and briars. A trail tunneled and wound around in the wasteland for a mile before opening onto a small sandy beach on the back side of the island. This was my private place. No one knew about it, not even Grandpa. I was going to show it to him one day, but he wouldn't let me.

"No. Everyone needs a secret place. I don't want you to show it to anyone, not even me," he'd said.

Bess knew the way without me guiding her. She stepped out of the thicket onto a narrow strip of sand. The beach edged a little lagoon, trapped from the main body of Currituck Sound by a bulkhead of cypress trees, deadfall, and cattails on two sides. A group of seagulls soared overhead. I could always count on the company of various birds and critters. They found good haven in this place.

On this particular day, a great blue heron rested on a rotting log that jutted out into the water and a red-winged blackbird flitted about in the cattails. I slid off my pony's back and eased down to sit in the sand near the trail, careful not to frighten off the heron.

Bess seemed to understand I wanted to be quiet, and she stood motionless beside me. The only sound was the rhythmic lap-lapping of the waves against the log.

I sat there a long time, thinking about everything I'd learned in the past two days. The idea of North Carolina joining the rest of the colonies in a revolt against King George was beginning to worry me. The taxes were unfair, considering we had no say in them whatsoever. I couldn't help thinking it was pretty laughable, though. Here everyone was in an uproar over taxes, yet the planters didn't consider their slaves, how they worked sunup to sundown on the plantations. Those slaves sure didn't get a say in anything. I didn't believe in slavery or revolution. All the mainlanders' talk about freedom was just talk, as far as I was concerned.

Mother, who taught me at an early age to read from the Bible, often read scriptures that told how God took care of us and knew everything. He knew how many hairs were on our heads and how many stars were in the sky. And he knew every grain of sand. Imagine that, I thought as I pushed my hand deep into the warm golden grains and lifted them up, letting them sift through my fingers. The breeze made them swirl, and they sparkled in the sun as they drifted back down to earth. I loved the beach. I could see why God would, too.

Losing track of the time was easy when I was thinking. I didn't know how long I'd been sitting there playing with the sand. Bess napped as she stood beside me. Before long, the warmth of the sun and the gentle noise of the waves lulled me to sleep, too.

The noise that woke me from my nap wasn't loud. Just a scurrying sound, like the one a mouse makes when he's exploring in the pantry. I opened my eyes, expecting to see a raccoon or some other critter. I didn't move, so's not to scare it off, whatever it was.

Well, it wasn't a raccoon. With a grunt, a wild boar walked out of the rushes, not thirty feet from Bess and me. He was the biggest hog I'd ever seen— he probably weighed three hundred pounds. His long tusks gleamed in the sunlight.

I remembered stories I'd heard Father and Mr. O'Reilly tell of boar attacks: dogs had been ripped apart by the razor-sharp tusks, and just last spring old Jim Williams was gored by a boar and lost his leg.

I waited, praying he wouldn't see us, until he turned toward the water's edge. I had to force myself to stay still and not make a sound. My first instinct was to run, but I knew I was no match for that monster's speed. The hairs on the back of my neck prickled and even though it was still warm, goose bumps worked their way up my arms. With relief, I watched the boar head to the lagoon. He stopped a few feet from the water's edge and pawed at the sand. It was only a miracle that my dear, sweet Bess did not bolt off, but stood still at my side.

When the hog dipped his ugly snout into the water, I jumped up, sprang onto Bess's back and pulled her around to face the trail. I didn't even have to squeeze my legs; Bess knew the danger, and she galloped down the path.

I could hear the wild pig snorting and crashing through the reeds behind us. The thorny briars grabbed at my clothes and a branch snapped me in the face. Then I remembered to duck and flatten out on Bess's back. My heart was pounding loud enough I could hear it.

"Oh, please, Bess, run like you've never run! Dear God in heaven, save us!"

When we got back to the sand dunes and out from the claws of vines and tree branches, I dared to look over my shoulder. The boar was nowhere in sight. Bess had outrun him. I offered another prayer, this time of thanks.

I pulled Bess down to a trot, and we crossed the dunes and rode the ocean beach toward home. I couldn't decide whether or not to tell I'd been chased by a wild boar. I was afraid if Mother knew, she'd never let me ride alone again. But what if I didn't tell anyone, and the boar attacked someone else? If that happened and someone was injured or killed, I'd have it on my conscience. I would have to tell.

I let Bess go with the herd, walked the rest of the way home, and managed to slip upstairs without being noticed. I closed my bedroom door without making a sound.

"Oh, my!" I looked in the mirror at my face. Streaks of red crisscrossed both my cheeks where the thorns had cut into my flesh. My shirt was torn and leaves were tangled in my hair. There would be no delaying it. I had to tell what had happened.

Chapter Seven

Mother noticed the scratches on my face right off, even though I tried to stay out of the light.

"Betsy, what has mommucked your face? Oh, dear, come let me look at you." Mother was near tears and I knew I could not escape her questioning. All the same, I saw no purpose in revealing how close I had come to an untimely end, since I was sure Mother would pack me off to Edenton if she knew the whole story.

So I plunged right in and started telling my tale, without revealing the location of my secret place, how close we'd been to the beast, or how fast it had chased us out of the woods. I told Mother Bess and I had gone for a ride on the sound shore when we saw the wild hog. "Bess and I saw the thing getting a drink. He was huge, and I turned Bess, and we ran away before he even had a chance to see us. I guess I just got scared. We were fine, really."

Mother put a salve on the scratches, and then I set the table for supper with extra places for Uncle John and Aunt Frances, who were staying over until the next day. The men would be going to hunt for the boar at dawn.

To make up for my sins of the afternoon, I played checkers with Johnny after supper. Later we sat on the front porch in Grandpa's swing. Fashioned from slats of cypress wood, it was simply a bench with a back, hung from the porch ceiling by two lengths of rope. You had to be careful not to swing too high or rock back and forth, or it would flip over backwards. All of the young'uns, including myself, had flipped over Grandpa's swing at one time or another.

That night Johnny and I just let it sway gently, pulling us into conversation.

"Were you scared?" Johnny was of course talking about my day's adventure with the wild boar. I couldn't pass up the chance to have a little fun. By the time I finished with him, he'd never ask to go riding with me again.

"Well, I'd be lying if I said I wasn't. I could hear him breathing and snorting, he was so close. He was about as big as Bess. Big and ugly and bloodthirsty. I could see his long, white tusks shining in the sun. They were about a foot long and sharp as razors. I could see blood dried up on the tips, probably where he'd gored somebody or something to death.

"Once Bess stumbled and I nearly fell off. If I had, he'd be eating me for supper tonight." I glanced sideways to see if the embellished version of my experience was having the desired effect. I saw Johnny shiver, which satisfied me.

"I'm sorry I left you behind, but sometimes I just have to get away from all that talking and be by myself.

"'Course, it all turned out for the best. If you'd come along, you might've fallen off and landed right in the path of that ole hog."

"I guess I'm glad you didn't invite me today," Johnny said.

"Oh, it wasn't all that bad. Bess took care of me. There's not a wild hog in the world that can outrun Bess."

We pushed the swing back into motion again. I pulled my left leg up into the seat, tucked it under my other leg, and leaned back so my hair hung over the back of the swing. The stars were out and a light breeze cooled the air.

Johnny broke the silence. "Papa says you Bankers have a good life here. He says sometimes he wishes he could live simple like you all."

"Really? I thought Aunt Frances and Uncle John considered us poor relatives, lower class."

"Well, maybe Mother thinks that way, but I think Papa would love to live like an islander. He has to worry about the crops and getting them to market. You know that hurricane flattened all the corn this summer. He spent days with the field workers trying to straighten it back up. With that new tax we probably won't earn enough to buy seed for next year's planting. That's what I heard him saying to Mr. Winslow."

Johnny stuck his foot out and pushed it against

the floor hard, making the swing twist back and forth. It felt like the fishing skiff in a rough sea.

I shivered; it was getting airish. "I didn't know. I guess I don't think about the hardship the Tea Act and all those other taxes cause folks who depend on trade overseas. We live from the sea and land here, but it's not simple. We work hard too."

"Papa says there will be an all-out war if King George doesn't repeal the taxes. He says people aren't going to stand still for it. That Lord Dunmore is a worry, Papa says." Johnny kicked the floor again.

"Will you please stop? You're making me sea-sick. Besides, I don't see why that ole coot would bother us. He's governor of Virginia—he's got nothing to do with North Carolina. And I'm sure things aren't as bad as you think. Why, just this afternoon Aunt Frances was inviting us to a big Christmas ball.

Surely she wouldn't be planning a party if we were about to be in a war." I planted both my feet on the porch floor and stopped the swing's rocking. We didn't say anything more.

I didn't have any notion that night what trouble that ole coot, Lord Dunmore, would end up causing me.

From the Diary of Rebecca Dowdy

November 30, 1774

The day started out pleasantly enough. Frances and Betsy and I knitted twenty-four hats. Betsy contributed at least three of those before I let her leave.

Her slow progress and the misery on her face as she tried to make her fingers work the knitting needles was more than I could bear. If I had known what was going to happen, I would never have excused her from our task.

Betsy was nearly killed today. She went off riding alone and was attacked by a wild boar. She tried to make it sound as if she had been in no danger, but the wounds on her face and arms tell me differently. Even the clothes she had been wearing are in shreds.

I told Josiah that was the last straw. I do not want Betsy out wandering this wild land alone ever again. These islands are swarming with swine and other creatures. This can be a dangerous and unforgiving place.

I just do not understand how Josiah can be so unconcerned. He tells me I cannot expect to keep her locked up inside this house all of the time. He was quick to point out that, had it not been for Bess, our daughter might not be alive tonight.

Not wanting to argue with my husband, I did not voice my thoughts. But I can write here that, were it not for that horse, my Betsy would never have been off in that wilderness in the first place.

I am going to insist that Betsy go stay a while in Edenton. It is high time she socialized with other young ladies her age and learned how to behave. I am sure she will enjoy the social life once she experiences it. And she needs further schooling. I have taught her all I can about numbers and the only book she reads is the Bible. Which is indeed a good book for her to read, but I want more for her. These islands only offer hard work, fish, storms, and sand. Sand is everywhere. It is in our clothing, in our beds, on the floors, even in our food. I am sick to death of sand.

Chapter Eight

December 1774

The incident with the wild boar was the last straw, as Mother put it. She sent me packing to stay with Aunt Frances for the winter season. The worst of it was I had to leave Bess behind. She was with foal. I'd seen her with a bay stallion last spring so I knew he was the father. He was a beauty, too. Bess was already getting a wide belly, and I knew she'd be better off staying with the herd. All the same, I missed her and the Banks.

From my bedroom window in Edenton I could see Albemarle Sound. If it wasn't for that, I believe I would have lost my mind right to begin with. Cypress trees drenched in beards of gray moss grew along the shore. Uncle John told me there were alligators in the swamp, but I didn't know that I believed him. Sometimes I saw geese flying over the sound. I wondered if they were coming from Currituck.

The winter season in Edenton was full of endless social events. Aunt Frances enthusiastically introduced me to Edenton society. The very first day she went right into having me try on some of her dresses while Rose, one of the house slaves, pinned them here and there to make them fit.

Rose turned out to be a talented seamstress. Aunt Frances was a good deal larger than I, but in two days' time the dresses were finished and Aunt Frances had invited some young ladies my age over for tea.

I found the tea tedious. Six giggling girls all talking about fashions and balls while we ate little sweetmeats and drank our tea, mint tea it was. Of course it wasn't polite to eat more than two sweets, which only made me hungrier.

It didn't seem fair that I had to attend a stupid tea while Johnny was out with Uncle John riding through the fields and checking on the crops. In high-society Edenton it seemed the boys had all the fun.

One of the girls, Martha Druman, was sister to Isaac Druman whose horse Bess had beaten in the race. Imagine my horror when she invited me to a foxhunt at their estate.

"I couldn't possibly accept," I said in my most polite voice. I would rather have taken a beating than gone to the Drumans' hunt. "I haven't any horse to ride." The idea of seeing Isaac Druman again made me want to throw up.

"Nonsense," she replied. "Isaac has a lovely mare you can borrow. I understand you are an excellent equestrian. I am sure you can handle her."

I looked at Aunt Frances, hoping she'd intervene and get me out of this invitation, but the pleased expression on her face proved I was hoping in vain. It occurred to me that she expected me to be thrilled with the plan, since she knew how much I loved to ride.

"Oh, she'd love that, Martha. How kind of you and your brother. Betsy loves to ride, and I know she misses her pony. Won't you just love to go, Betsy?" Aunt Frances smiled at me and waited for me to answer.

"Yes," I said. "Yes, ma'am. Thank you very much." There was no way to avoid it; the following week I was going to a foxhunt.

Three or four days passed before I had the chance to explore the beach that bordered Uncle John and Aunt Frances's land. A cart path led from the house to the sound. The path had fields on both sides for a half a mile and then it wound through some woods. As I walked along, squirrels chattered at me for invading their territory. Just as I was about to step into the open, I saw a deer at the water's edge. Hearing my footsteps, she raised her head and turned her ears this way and that. I stood still as I could, but she flagged her tail and bounded into the woods.

The trees shielded me from the wind and the sun was warm. I sat down on a log that lay near the water. It was peaceful and I knew this would be a spot I would visit often.

"Well, Mother," I said out loud, "here I am in Edenton. I miss you and Father and Bess. I think it is Aunt Frances's intention to keep me so busy I won't have time to think of home, but nothing can take my thoughts away from the sandy beaches of Currituck Banks."

Realizing how foolish I must have sounded talking to Mother, who was miles away, I looked around to make sure Johnny wasn't hiding in the bushes listening. Satisfied that I was alone, I trailed my fingers in the water and thought about upcoming events. I was not looking forward to either the ball or the foxhunt, but I could not devise a way of avoiding them. I thought perhaps I could pretend to be sick.

Just as that idea came into my mind, a wave slapped up against the log and made me remember a day Grandpa and I were out fishing in his skiff. As we drifted along, waves slapped up against the hull, making that same sound.

I remembered him saying, "Sometimes you have to do what you really don't want to do, just because it's the right thing. It takes courage sometimes to do a simple thing. But once you get up the courage and do it, you find it was easier than you thought. It's just thinking about it that makes it so hard."

"I guess this is one of those times. I'll just do it and be done with it. I can't disappoint Aunt Frances or Mother," I said out loud. "And no matter what kind of old nag Isaac Druman sends over tomorrow, I'll ride it."

My mind had already conjured up an old, gray, sway-backed horse limping down the carriage drive.

Chapter Nine

Aunt Frances was more excited than I had ever seen a grown person. Poor Rose was called upon to alter another gown for me, as well as redo one for Aunt Frances. She took bows off of one dress and put them on the other. Then she trimmed the bodice with velvet ribbon and little pearl buttons. I had to admit the gown was quite beautiful.

It was not easy for me to get used to hooped skirts and all those petticoats. I found it especially difficult to sit down in a hooped skirt. Aunt Frances had me practice going up and down the stairs, showing me how to hold my skirt just high enough not to trip on it, but not too high. She said I must not show my ankles. I thought all her high-society rules were silly, but I did have good enough manners not to tell her so.

Next, Aunt Frances instructed Rose to make me a riding habit.

"Why can't I ride the way I do at home? I just wear my normal clothes and pull my skirt up between my legs and jump on."

"Oh, heavens above, no, young lady. You cannot just hike up your skirt and ride. And you must use a lady's sidesaddle. Riding astride is considered vulgar by genteel folk."

The hunt ball, which took place on the eve of the hunt, was a lavish affair. The ballroom was huge. I don't believe I'd ever seen such a large room. All the ladies' dresses were so colorful and the candlelight gave everything a golden glow. We were all dressed in twice-made gowns, but it didn't matter a bit. In fact, the women of Edenton considered the dresses a matter of pride because of the boycott they were observing.

The folks in Chowan County were fond of putting on great feasts, and I must say they upheld their reputation that night. A long table covered with food and a large bowl of punch stood at one end of the room, and the musicians were stationed at the other.

The table was covered with a white linen cloth and in its center was a large silver bowl piled high with fruit. Flanking either side of the centerpiece were platters of sliced ham, various pies and cakes, bowls of salted and roasted pecans and peanuts, preserves, and much more than I can remember.

Isaac himself greeted us. I gave a polite curtsy and tried to keep the blood from rushing to my face, but a twinkle in his eye showed he'd noticed my blushing.

Then his sister swept me away, much to my

relief, and introduced me to a group of three girls. One of them was Penelope Barker's cousin, and the other two were named Alice and Margaret. I had met Alice and Margaret at the tea. They were giggling behind their fans and watching Isaac with an astonishing amount of interest.

The fiddlers started playing, and suddenly my companions began fluttering their fans nervously and whispering. "Here he comes. Oh, do you think he is going to ask one of us to dance?" said Alice. Then she giggled again.

"It's you he's looking at, Betsy," said Margaret, grinning mischievously.

"What?" I said.

That was all I had a chance to say, because there he was, taking my hand, smiling in the most charming way, and leading me onto the ballroom floor.

Chapter Ten

At the break of dawn, one of Isaac's field hands came with my horse. Uncle John, Johnny, and I left for the hunt shortly afterward. Aunt Frances no longer rode, so she didn't go with us, but planned to meet us later at the breakfast.

The mare was a beautiful gray, with dark luminous eyes, nothing like the nag I had imagined. She pranced lightly, as though her feet never touched the ground. She made me think of a leaf dancing on a breeze. Her name was Bell, and I loved her immediately.

The early morning sun sparkled through the frost that coated the beige grasses and foxtails growing at the edge of the fields. The air had a bite to it and was full of the fragrance of nuts and earth and spices. Uncle John, Johnny, and I trotted our horses across a cornfield in an easterly direction. The Druman estate was within easy hacking distance.

As we rode along I thought about the last night's ball, where I had danced every dance. Of course Uncle John and Johnny both asked me to dance; then there were Thomas Knowles and Samuel Roper and Alice's brother, James, and the last, Isaac again. He was a much better dancer than he was a jockey. I had to give him his due.

I could only hope the day's hunt would turn out as pleasantly as the ball. I'd truly had the most exhilarating time since my arrival in Edenton.

Thank goodness I'd had a chance to practice riding in Aunt Frances's sidesaddle before the day of the hunt. It surely took some getting used to. I wasn't worried by the time we got to the Drumans' estate; Bell and I were getting along just fine.

Isaac and Martha rode down the carriage drive to meet us. "How do you like Bell?" he asked.

"Oh, she is beautiful," I said. I wanted to bite my tongue for sounding so eager. Forcing my voice down to sound polite, the way Aunt Frances had taught me in our etiquette lessons, I said, "Thank you for letting me borrow her."

"I raised her myself. She's a good hunter and never hesitates at a fence. I hope you will enjoy her and the hunt."

"The air is right for it. The hounds can pick out the scent well on a frosty morning like the one we have today," said Uncle John.

"Good morning, Betsy," Martha greeted me. "Oh my, you look marvelous! Doesn't she look beautiful, Isaac?" Martha turned to her brother and smiled.

"Yes, indeed, you look smashing."

My riding habit was made of dark green velvet. The caplet and cuffs were edged with rabbit's fur. My hat had a green plume. The hat seemed silly, but Aunt Frances had insisted I wear it.

"Thank you. Rose is a wonderful seamstress." I tried to be gracious, but my cheeks were burning with embarrassment.

The hounds spilled out into the courtyard, raising a ruckus with their baying. Soon the huntsman blew his horn, and we set off across the fields. The dogs picked up the scent of the fox, and the hunt was on in earnest.

I learned that a fox is a crafty animal. He can swim and climb a tree in addition to circling and backtracking. The hounds soon found it was not an easy task to keep up with their prey. Several times we had to stop and wait for the hounds to pick the scent back up after being "outfoxed." Whenever that happened the huntsman circled the hounds around the spot where the fox was last seen. Soon the hounds would start baying again and the chase would resume.

I heeded Uncle John's advice to be quiet and stay behind, off to the side of the pack. I didn't want to distract the dogs from their job. Bell was as sure-footed through muddy swamp as she was on solid ground. She took the few fences we had to cross with such ease that I began to feel very secure in the sidesaddle.

After a long morning of chase, the fox carried the hounds into an area near the forest that bordered the sound. We followed hounds and fox through a patch of tall reeds. Trying to stay off to the side of the pack, I guided Bell closer to the line of trees. Ahead of me I could see that the fox was taking a winding path through the reeds in hopes of confusing the dogs.

I saw a fallen tree in Bell's way and tried to figure out if we could go around it. Before I'd decided, Bell gathered herself, haunches crouched, and sprang over the trunk. Unfortunately, her leap caught me unawares and sent me sprawling into the muck. The mare stopped immediately and stood over me with a most quizzical look in her eyes.

I was at the back of the hunting field with Johnny behind me. He pulled up his mount as soon as he saw me take my fall. Surely I was a most hilarious sight, but poor Johnny had the good sense not to laugh, not until I started to giggle myself.

"Are you hurt?" he asked.

"No, except for my pride. I hope no one else saw me." I looked around, but everyone was well up ahead.

Being a good gentleman, Johnny dismounted and helped me to my feet. I looked down at the beautiful riding habit, which was now covered in mud. The vision of poor Rose sewing into the night to finish it in time sobered me right away.

"Oh, my goodness. I have ruined my clothes. Johnny, where is my hat?" I felt the top of my head as if it might have got back on somehow.

"Here it is, Betsy. I don't see the feather, though." Johnny bent over and picked up a soggy green thing that no longer in any way resembled a hat.

I felt like crying and probably would have, had I not noticed a rider coming our way, backtracking to find what had become of Johnny and me.

"Help me quick," I said. "I must get back to the hunt. I will be mortified if I have interrupted anything." I knew that stopping the hunt was a major offense in fox hunting.

Johnny gave me a quick leg up and remounted his pony. We trotted to meet the rider. It was Isaac.

"Is everything all right back here?" he questioned.

"Yes," I answered, trying to smooth my jacket and keep my face from flushing. I achieved neither.

"She took a tumble, but she's just fine," Johnny said, "We'll catch up, don't worry."

"Yes, I'm fine. Go ahead back to the hunt. Bell and I will catch up."

Isaac looked hard at us, as if trying to decide what would be the proper thing to do, then cantered back to join the others.

I would have loved nothing better than to be swallowed up by the earth, but instead Johnny and I trotted on through the reeds to follow the hunt. For the first time Johnny had been a help and not a hindrance. I winked at him and he flashed a big grin.

By the time we caught up with the rest of the party, the fox had taken refuge in a thicket of blackberry brambles. The hunters beat the bushes with their sticks. I cringed when the fox ran out and the dogs killed him. Even with my eyes turned away, I could hear the snarling and barking of the hounds until they finally killed the fox.

The hunters were in a jubilant mood as they rode back to the Druman estate, but I did not share in the merriment. I had hoped that the fox would escape with his life, which Aunt Frances had assured me was most often the case. I could not see the point in hunting foxes to their death, even if they did raid the chicken houses. I made up my mind I would never attend another hunt.

When I rode into the stable yard and dismounted, a young boy led Bell away to be groomed and fed a hot mash. Martha hustled me upstairs, where she asked Daisy, the housemaid, to brush the mud off my riding habit. Then Martha helped me adjust my hair. She declared my hat beyond repair. Finally, I looked into the hall mirror and was satisfied that I was somewhat presentable for the breakfast. Perhaps I could stand behind Aunt Frances and no one would notice what a mess I was.

From the Diary of Rebecca Dowdy

December 18, 1774

I received a letter from Betsy today. Just as I thought, she is having a wonderful time going to teas and balls, and even a hunt. I was shocked when she wrote that she took a fall. Frances assures me my Betsy was not hurt. She did not hold up the hunt, but remounted her horse and carried on as if nothing at all had happened. Betsy is such an excellent rider, but she's not familiar with riding aside.

Isaac Druman hosted the foxhunt. Since he and Betsy know one another from that infamous horse race, I just hope she behaved in a ladylike manner. I have the most awful vision of Betsy sticking out her tongue at him, or something vulgar like that. I pray she did not.

Betsy did not make any mention of her studies, but Frances wrote that she is very smart and doing well with her schooling. Of course that is not news to me. I have always known Betsy is as smart as she is beautiful.

News has come that the political situation is worsening in the north. I do wish they would come to a peaceful settlement. It is horrible to think of people losing their lives for the sake of tax money. I know they say it is for freedom, but I fear the colonies may have bitten off more than they can chew.

I miss having Betsy at home. I did not realize what good company she was until I deprived myself of her presence. And I know Annie must miss her help with the livestock. Well, so be it. Milking a cow is no task for a lady.

Chapter Eleven

Spring 1775

I expected to spend a long and miserable winter in Edenton, but the time passed much faster than I'd anticipated. Aunt Frances saw to it that I had little time for pining, keeping me in a perpetual whirlwind of social engagements. In addition, I had my studies. I enjoyed math, but detested needlework and etiquette lessons. Johnny had his lessons separate from me. That made me wonder what fun I might be missing.

Mother and Father were not able to come for the Christmas ball because a nor'easter kept them from leaving the island. It was the first Christmas I'd ever spent away from my family at Chapel Field. I was more than a little homesick. Aunt Frances did all she could to distract me from my melancholy and I did my best not to let her see how sad I felt. Mother and Father did come visit later and that lifted my spirits. We had a grand time and exchanged our gifts and had a nice tea. They left the next day because Father couldn't leave the fishing nets for O'Reilly to tend all alone.

When my homesickness was too much to bear, I often slipped away to the small beach behind Uncle John's farm. There I was able to listen to the waves licking at the narrow strip of sand. If I sat very quietly, it was not unusual for me to see a raccoon or even a deer come to the water's edge for a drink. The little beach on the Albemarle was a peaceful place for meditation. Still, it wasn't home.

I made one last visit to the little beach the afternoon before I was to go home. It was late evening and the sun was low in the sky, coloring the clouds a soft pink. I sat on my log, deep in thoughts of seeing Mother and Father again, and of course my dear Bess.

My thoughts had carried me away, and I didn't hear the hooves on the dirt path. When Isaac Druman spoke, I nearly fell off my log.

"Oh, my goodness! What are you thinking to sneak up on me that way?" I jumped up and brushed the leaves off my skirt.

Isaac dismounted, landing lightly on his feet, took off his hat, and made an exaggerated bow. He gave me a devilish grin. "A thousand pardons, dear lady. I did not realize you were so deep in thought, or I would have called out to you."

I was sure he was teasing me. I decided to play along and act as if I believed him to be earnest.

"Oh, it is quite all right. I was thinking of home, and how glad I will be to see my beautiful Chapel Field once again." I tried to tell if he was smirking or smiling at me and decided it didn't matter. Soon I would be home, far away from Isaac Druman, who seemed so amused by me.

"I will miss you, Betsy Dowdy. You have been like a breath of sweet, fresh air among all these stuffy society ladies," Isaac said, looking straight into my eyes. I was certain this time he wasn't kidding, which made me more uncomfortable than his taunting had.

"You are most gracious to say such kind things." I stood up, ready to walk back to the house. Now I didn't know what to think of Isaac. Worst of all, I didn't know what to think of how he made me feel. Since the dance and the fox hunt, my disdain for him had melted away, to be replaced by an unfamiliar emotion. What did I know about love at that young age? I loved my parents, and the wild horses of Currituck Banks, but I knew nothing about romance.

"Oh please. I am afraid I have interrupted you, and now you won't watch the sunset. Stay, and I promise to stand quietly by while you enjoy the view."

"No, I must really get back before dark. I don't want to worry Aunt Frances."

"She knows I am here with you. I stopped by the house to call on you. Your Aunt Frances told me I'd find you here. But if you insist, let me give you a ride."

Isaac got back on his horse, then leaned down and reached his hand out to me. I don't know what came over me, but I accepted his hand and next thing I knew I was sitting astride right behind Isaac Druman on his fancy black stallion.

We didn't leave the shore right away. Isaac guided Diablo out into the water until the horse was chest-deep. I reached down, pulled off my shoes, and let my feet dangle in the water. There we waited until the whole sky was awash in gold and red. The colors were reflected in the sound, so that for a moment we were a part of the sunset. Then Isaac turned the stallion around, and we trotted back up the cart path to the house. He dismounted and gave me his hand while I slid off the horse's back.

"May I come to call on you at Chapel Field?" he asked.

"Yes, of course, you will be welcome to visit us any time." I turned and stumbled up the steps to the front door in my haste. Was Isaac Druman asking to court me? That thought was downright scary.

I didn't sleep a wink that night. The moon rose and positioned itself just outside my window, casting its pale, white light across my bed. My heart seemed to quiver every time I thought of the evening's events at the sound shore. I had never felt like I did while sitting behind Isaac watching that glorious sunset. I'd been warm all over, even though there had been a chill to the air. Even as I lay in my bed I could still feel that warmth and smell the fragrance of tobacco and wool and horses that came from Isaac's clothing.

I couldn't help but smile a little to think what Mother would say if she had seen me riding double with Isaac Druman. I was sure what I had done was very unladylike.

The next morning I felt a mixture of emotions. I was excited that I was going home, but I wanted to see Isaac again. Father had written that Bess was due to have her foal any day. I prayed she'd wait until I got there. My thoughts of Isaac drifted away as I gathered my things for the trip. I did not intend to tell anyone about that evening on the beach.

Looking out the rippled panes of my bedroom window, I saw the driver bring the carriage up the drive. I hurried downstairs, with Rose right behind me carrying what baggage I couldn't hold.

Aunt Frances had a basket packed with ham biscuits, boiled eggs and pumpkin pie for our trip. Uncle John would take me as far as the Church Island landing. There, Daddy would meet me in the fishing skiff. Johnny accompanied Uncle John and me, hoping for some adventure along the way.

"We could see a bear or even Indians!" he said.

The carriage swayed and bumped as the horses plodded down the muddy road. Spring rains had left water standing axle-deep in places, and the ruts left by wagons that had gone before made the going treacherous. Molly, Uncle John's carriage horse, did her job well and pulled us through. Her sure-footedness amazed me.

Uncle John stopped by the tavern in Elizabeth City to find news to carry to the Banks.

"We are headed toward our independence," said a man who overheard my uncle's inquiries.

"Aye, speaker Harvey has declared we should have a convention of our own, without the governors," the keeper of the tavern said. "It is a troubling time we're in, it is."

I sipped my hot cider, wrapping both hands around the cup for warmth. Soon I would be back on the sandy beaches of home. There I could listen to the gulls laughing and the constant pounding of the surf. It was all I could do to mind my manners and not nag Uncle John to leave, I so wanted to continue the journey to see my family and Bess.

The discussion grew longer as the men exchanged stories of the injustices inflicted upon the colonies by King George. I was afraid they'd never stop talking. What could a few farmers in the wild backcountry of North Carolina do about the King and things that were happening in faraway Boston, Massachusetts?

"Mother says you are sweet on Isaac Druman." Johnny's comment almost made me choke on my cider.

"Don't be daft." I felt the redness spread across my cheeks. Could he have known about the night before? Had that rascal been hiding in the woods watching?

"You're blushing, Betsy Dowdy! And she says he's sweet on you, too."

"I really doubt Aunt Frances would discuss such things with you, Jonathan! You can just hush right this minute. I don't want anyone starting rumors because they've overheard my addled cousin making up tales."

"Oh, she didn't tell me, but I heard her say those very words to Mrs. Winslow when they were standing out on the front porch yesterday. Mother says by next winter she just bets he asks for your hand."

"He can ask all he wants, which I doubt seriously he does, but I have no intention of becoming a mainlander nor could I bear to leave my ponies. The man who marries me must love the sea as much as I. Anyway, I see no reason why I should want to marry at all."

"Well, he loves his horses. You know he has the best breeding stock in all of Carolina. And how would you know if he loves the sea or not? You've hardly spoken a word to him. When we had Isaac and Martha over for dinner last week you sat there mum as a corpse."

"I just couldn't think of anything to say. We have so little in common. Isaac sweet on me? He can have the pick of any lady in Edenton. What would he want with a islander like me?"

Johnny was distracted by laughter coming from a group across the room playing a game of darts, and I sipped my cider in silence until Uncle John summoned us to get back into the carriage.

I was sure Johnny didn't know about Isaac's visit on the beach, or he would have teased me about it. Besides, I didn't believe Aunt Frances had said anything of the kind, about Isaac being sweet on me. Johnny was just trying to get my goat. As far as he knew Isaac Druman hadn't given me a second thought, not since I fell off his mare and showed up at the hunt breakfast covered in mud. Then I remembered what Isaac had said about me being different than the other ladies in Edenton, but I dismissed the thought. Isaac had just been teasing. Yes, that was all. He'd just been teasing me.

Chapter Twelve

We reached Church Island landing about three o'clock in the afternoon, as planned. Father was waiting with the skiff. I couldn't begin to tell how happy I was to see him. As we embraced, I filled my lungs with his salty, fishy smell and felt at home at once.

"What news do you have, John?" Father inquired.

"We are traveling toward independence, Josiah," answered my uncle.

"What does that mean? King George isn't going to let us out from under his thumb just because we say so." I could read the concern on Father's face.

"No, he won't let us go without a fight, but he has underestimated our resolve. We will fight or die!"

"John, those are hard words. Do you think it will really come to that?"

"It already has. Eight were killed in battle at Lexington just this past week. The British are trying to destroy our supplies. They marched on to Concord, but news of the killings in Lexington had spread. By the time the redcoats got to Concord, the people were ready. They forced the British troops clear back to Boston."

All that talk of fighting was alarming. When my uncle told Father that nearly 300 British soldiers and ninety colonists had lost their lives in the battle at Concord, a dark look came over Father's face. He clenched his fist and cursed. Seeing his reaction frightened me. All I wanted was to go home, where Lexington and Concord seemed very far away and my island was safe from redcoats. Father packed my bags into the skiff, and we pushed off, waving good-bye to Uncle John and Johnny until my arm tired and they disappeared on the horizon.

"How is Bess, Father? She didn't have her foal yet, did she?" I asked.

"Not when I left, she hadn't. But it will be any hour, I think. She's moved away from the herd, has been off to herself for two days now. Maybe she's waiting for you to come home," he said with a smile.

"I can't wait!" For the moment I forgot the talk of battles and taxes and such. All I was worried about was coming ashore and coming home to Chapel Field, my family and Black Bess.

I wanted to run straight across the dunes and find my little mare, but I walked home with Father.

Before we reached the front door, Mother came running down the steps, her arms stretched out.

She held on to me so tightly I could barely breathe. Then she let me go. Holding me at arms' length, she looked hard at me a moment and said, "Welcome back, Betsy Dowdy! My, I have missed you, daughter."

"And I have you, Mother. I have missed these islands and my family more than you can guess."

"Yes, I know. Now, take your things up to your room. Then off with you. I know you are anxious to go see that Bess of yours. Who knows, she may have something to show you by now."

I gave her another hug and a kiss. "Yes, thank you, Mother. I can hardly wait to see her, and if she's had her foal."

"Fine, dear. I will have you some tea when you come back." Mother had a wistful look about her, as if she'd lost something. Before I turned to go up the stairs I saw her wipe away a tear from the corner of her eye.

Chapter Thirteen

I waited until I was out of Mother's sight before running toward Penny Hill. As I climbed to the top, my feet sank deep into the soft sand. When I reached the crest, I caught my breath and scanned the area for Bess. Her herd was grazing in a clearing near the sound, but Bess wasn't anywhere to be seen. I called to her and waited for her answering whinny, but all I heard were the ocean waves crashing against the sandy beach.

My skin prickled and my heart pounded as I walked down the back side of the hill where I was sure I would find Bess. I knew that once she made up her mind to have her foal, it wouldn't take long. Grandpa had explained that to me. It only took a mare about half an hour to give birth, not like the stories I'd overheard Mother and Aunt Frances tell about women taking hours and hours to have their babies. If I didn't hurry I'd miss the whole thing.

I walked slowly, careful not to make a noise. Soon I was there. A clump of myrtle bushes and pine trees grew at the bottom of the dune. The limbs of the trees hung low, and vines twisted and twined their way from the ground up into the branches, forming a wall. It was one of Bess's favorite resting places, offering shelter from wind and rain.

I was right. Bess was lying on the soft carpet of pine straw. She was wet with sweat. When she saw me, she started to stand up.

"Shhh, shhh, girl. Don't get up, it's all right, girl." I kneeled beside her and stroked her neck. She relaxed a little, stretched her neck out, and rubbed it against the sweet-smelling pine needles. Then she moaned, and I felt her muscles tense under my hand. It wouldn't be long before Bess's baby was here. I saw a tiny hoof, then another, then a tiny black nose. Minutes later the most beautiful black foal I'd ever seen made his appearance. He was still covered in a thin, clear membrane from the neck down.

Grandpa once told me that if the membrane didn't break clear of the foal's nose, it would smother. Usually by the time the foal was born the membrane was broken. If not, the mare helped by licking it away. He also told me that the mare and foal would need a few minutes to rest.

"Getting born is hard work, both for the mother and the baby," he'd said. I hoped Grandpa was watching from heaven and could see Bess's baby.

"Oh, Bess! You have the most beautiful foal," I whispered. Tears welled up in my eyes and trickled down my cheeks. I was so proud of my Bess, and I was sorely aware that I stood in the presence of a miracle.

Bess turned her head and stretched out her neck toward the wet, shiny, black form lying behind her. I stepped back out of her way so she could meet her new baby and wiped my face dry with the back of my hand. Bess made sweet, soft nickering sounds as she nuzzled her foal. Little kisses, I thought.

While the mother and baby lay resting, I took a good close look. I wanted to be sure everything was all right. The first thing I noticed was Bess's baby was a boy, a handsome little colt. He was breathing and I guessed that was a good sign. He was pure black from head to toe, except for a small white star on his forehead.

"Star," I said. "Let's name him Star."

Bess looked at me as if in agreement. Then she stood up, nickered, and nudged at Star until he tried to stand, too. It took three or four hilarious attempts before he was standing on his own wobbly legs. Then he collapsed back onto the pine needle bed. I laughed at the expression on his face. It was like he just couldn't figure out how to make those legs work.

"Here, let me help you," I said. I put my arms around him and lifted. He wasn't very heavy. His body was still damp, but warm. I got him on his feet and steadied him for a few moments while he found his balance. Grandpa was probably frowning now. I knew Star didn't really need my help; I was just being impatient. I couldn't wait to get my hands on him.

Now Bess was trying to line him up so he could nurse, but he was looking in all the wrong places. I laughed again.

"Come on, breakfast is right back here." I guided his muzzle to Bess's teats, which by now

were dripping milk. Finally Star found the right spot and started sucking noisily.

Bess seemed perfectly happy now. I sat down on the ground and watched the mother and baby. Bess was going to be a good mother, I could tell that. I would have liked to stay and watch them all day, but I remembered my own mother and knew she was waiting to see me and give me a proper homecoming. I gave Bess and Star a hug.

"I'll be back soon with visitors, so don't you two go anywhere," I whispered in Bess's ear, giving her one more pat before I started home.

I couldn't help grinning to think how shocked Mother would be when she learned I'd just witnessed Black Bess give birth to her baby. She worried enough that I helped feed the chickens and pigs. I decided not to tell her I'd seen the whole thing.

From the Diary of Rebecca Dowdy

April 28, 1775

My Betsy came home today. She is not the same Betsy who left. It is not just how she looks, which is quite the young woman—her hair was styled in a new coiffeur and her fingernails clean, and she was wearing a pretty dress decorated with pearl buttons down the front. But even when she came back downstairs in her old Osnabrig, she was different.

It is her inner self that has changed. She's no longer a little girl. Well, it is what I wanted, for her to learn to be a lady. While I am happy to see her growing up, I am going to miss my spirited daughter.

One thing is for sure; she has not lost her love of horses. Black Bess had her foal just minutes after Betsy found her at the edge of a live oak grove, behind

127

Penny Hill. Of course, Betsy didn't tell me she'd witnessed the actual birth of the foal, but I could tell from the sparkle in her eyes she'd had an extraordinary experience. It makes me laugh, the things that girl thinks I don't know.

Once all was well, Betsy came running home to have us come take a look. The colt is black like his mother, with a white star on his forehead. Betsy has named him Star. By the time we got there, he was already running and bucking. He knew not to stray far from his mother, and if she considered him too adventuresome, she would call him back to her side. Then she would make a big display of checking him over, nuzzling and sniffing him head to toe. Betsy is beside herself with delight.

Josiah brought home disturbing news from John today. The struggle between the colonies and King

George has become intense, and I think it will be only a matter of time before our men in Carolina are called to arms.

Chapter Fourteen

I spent spring on the island helping Mother and Annie with the garden. Mother and I started having afternoon tea. That seemed to really please her. Having tea was one way to let her know I had learned some niceties while I was in Edenton, and it gave us a chance to make conversation. I'd not ever really taken time for that before.

Fishing with Father and O'Reilly was another thing I'd missed while in Edenton. I went whenever I could. I loved going out in the skiff. One day we caught a net full of bluefish.

"A good catch this is, Mr. Dowdy," said O'Reilly as we began to haul in the net. It was so heavy I thought we might not be able to pull it in, but the three of us worked hard and finally the fish were in the boat. Then we went about sorting out the blues from the trash fish. Seagulls swarmed behind us, diving down to catch the small fish we threw overboard. A sand shark we threw back, and several spiny blowfish. But most of the catch was blues, and big ones at that.

"Miss Betsy, did I ever tell you 'bout the time I met old Blackbeard himself?" Mr. O'Reilly was fond of spinning yarns.

"Yes sir, you have. But I love that story, so please tell us again."

"Well, you know, afore the inlet filled in, he used to hide back behind this island. He'd sail the Queen Anne's Revenge, that's what he named his ship, and anchor just up behind the dunes until it was safe to sail back out to sea.

"See, Mr. Edward Teach, that's his real name, had a good many friends in Virginia and Carolina.

He paid good money for them, he did! So he was pretty safe at Currituck Banks. I was just a lad when the old pirate stomped these grounds. I'll never forget the night he came to dinner, at my father's invitation.

"I was quaking in my boots, I can tell you that, but he was every bit the gentleman. He gave me this gold coin, saying, 'Sonny, there's plenty more buried right here on your island. Find it and it's yours. Ye'll be a rich man.'"

O'Reilly kept the coin around his neck; he'd drilled a hole in it and strung it on a piece of fish net cordage.

Every time I heard Mr. O'Reilly tell that story, my heart did an extra beat. The thought of the infamous pirate sailing in these waters and burying treasure among the dunes of Currituck Banks was intriguing.

"I've dug and dug, but never found the pirate's gold. You can believe it is here somewhere on this island. Spanish gold, a chest full of it."

Star grew like a weed, getting strong and fast, taking after Bess. I visited them every day, so he would be tame. He would let me come up to pet him and feed him treats.

After a few weeks Bess and her baby rejoined the herd. It didn't take Star long to become independent and venture away from his mother. I delighted in watching his antics with the other foals. A little chestnut filly was his favorite play-mate. They challenged each other in games of chase, bucking and rearing, and then hid behind their mothers whenever they needed to rest.

Watching Bess wean Star was sad, and funny. I felt sorry for him, knowing he couldn't understand why his mother was rejecting him. The funny part was how he'd try to sneak up on her to nurse. He was pretty smart in his attempts, but she'd have no part of it. She knew she couldn't provide nourishment for both of them with winter coming. Whenever he'd approach, Bess would kick or run him away with her teeth bared. He was persistent for a few days, but being mighty independent anyway, he soon drifted away from his mother to join a small group of other weanlings.

Every afternoon just before sundown, after the sea breeze had chased away the heat, I rode Bess with Star following along. In truth, he usually galloped up ahead of us, interrupting sandpipers from their search for supper as he went. His little hoof prints beat a path in the wet sand as the sun cast its setting glow on the whitecaps, turning them gold and rose. I could imagine him all grown up, leading his herd down the beach.

A feeling of oneness always came over me on these rides. Thoughts of the conflict between the colonies and our mother country disappeared into the gray line between sky and sea. Surely, nothing could take that feeling away from me. I swore I would never leave these islands again, not for Isaac Druman, nor my mother, nor the King of England.

And so I spent the summer and fall living an islander's idyllic existence. The revolt against Britain seemed safely far away. I paid little attention to the bits and pieces of news Father received from the mainland, until one December evening when Mr. Sam Jarvis returned from a visit to Church Island.

Chapter Fifteen

December 1775

Mr. Jarvis came over after supper on a breezy December night. He brought with him a *Virginia Gazette*, and read an article to us that described how Lord Dunmore had captured Portsmouth, Virginia, leaving Norfolk defenseless. Dunmore was quoted as saying, "I really believe we should reduce this colony to a proper sense of their duty." I didn't know the governor of Virginia, but he did not sound like a gentleman.

Mr. Jarvis read on that George Washington said Lord Dunmore should be crushed, that if the colonies were going to survive they had to get Dunmore out of Norfolk.

According to Mr. Jarvis, Dunmore had barricaded Great Bridge. Tar, turpentine, shingles and the other forestry products that were shipped from Carolina had to cross Great Bridge to get to the port in Norfolk. Father agreed that the fate of Carolina depended on being able to sell our goods over the sea.

I knew the fact that we were about to be cut off from the world and unable to sell our goods was a serious problem, but what Mr. Jarvis said next sent a cold chill down my spine.

"Dunmore has burned homes and crops in Virginia. Why, he even stole all the gold and silver he could get his hands on and slaughtered the livestock and horses."

"Horses! Did you say he killed horses?" I was horrified.

"Yes, Miss Betsy. I am sorry to say so. I hear

tell the man has pillaged and destroyed everything in his path. Without horses we have no way to get supplies to our troops. If he is not stopped, he will move right on down the coast to North and South Carolina. Nothing will go unscathed."

"Well, surely he won't want to bother with our Banker ponies. He will have to get past me first!" I must have sounded overwrought by then, because that is when Mother said she thought it was time I went to bed.

I went upstairs like Mother said, but sleep would not come to me. My heart pounded and my chest hurt. That heinous Lord Dunmore wanted to kill our horses. What if they couldn't stop him at Great Bridge?

"What they need are more recruits," Mr. Jarvis had said. "General William Skinner has over a hundred men in Hertford, but I doubt the news has reached them yet. I'm going to sail up the Albemarle to the mainland tomorrow and pass the news along. The post won't be able to reach Edenton, Dunmore has seen to that. I just hope it won't be too late."

Too late, I kept thinking over and over. *What if it is too late and what if Lord Dunmore does come down our coast? What if he kills the ponies? What if he kills Black Bess and Star? He would have to kill me first.*

I could hear the wind blowing up a breeze outside my window. *What if a storm blew in and Mr. Jarvis couldn't sail to Perquimans and warn General Skinner of what was about to happen? What if Dunmore sailed his warship into Currituck Sound and burned our house? What if he slaughtered Bess and the rest of the Banker herd?*

139

That is when the thought entered my head—it was me who loved the ponies more than anyone. It was me Bess had trusted enough to carry on her back up and down the beach, through the woods, me she swam with in the sound, and me she won the race for. And it was me who had to save her. I had to save the Bankers from Lord Dunmore and his pirates.

Chapter Sixteen

I listened to Mother and Father say their good-byes to Mr. Jarvis and the crunch of his footsteps as he walked down the oyster shell path.

After all was quiet in the house, I wrote a note to Mother and laid it on my pillow.

"I have gone to carry the news of Lord Dunmore to General Skinner," was all it explained.

I put on my woolen stockings and leather slippers and slipped into my shift and wool skirt and bodice. Next, I folded a second change of clothes and wrapped them in my oilskin cloak and tied it about my shoulders. Holding my breath as I opened the door a crack, I looked into the hall. All was quiet. I tippy-toed down the hall, careful to step over the creaky board near the head of the staircase.

I was tempted to slide down the banister, but thought better of it. I might fall and wake the household. Each step seemed to groan with alarming noisiness. Finally, I reached the bottom.

Once I was outside, I hurried toward the dunes, avoiding the shell path. I ran to the hammock where the ponies usually spent the night. I could see them in the moonlight. Black Bess stood dozing. As soon as I whistled she perked up her ears in my direction. I whistled again and she came trotting toward me. She nudged my hand and I felt a pang of guilt. In my haste I had forgotten to bring an ear of corn.

"I promise, Bess, you get me to Skinner in time and you'll get your fill of corn!" I told her. Bess was a forgiving horse and let me slip on her halter, dropping her head and putting her nose through the loop.

I mounted up and we trotted out of the dunes and headed south, down the beach. I waited until we were well out of sight of the house before I guided Bess to the back side of the island.

Trying not to think of how airish it was, I urged my pony into the moonlit waters of Currituck Sound. I gave a silent prayer of thanks that it was an ebb tide. The water would not be more than two feet deep until we reached the middle. There a channel, at least three hundred yards wide, ran deeper, and we would have to swim until it shallowed out once again. After that we could wade through until we reached the shore of Church Island. Were it not for the cold, swimming the sound would be an easy task. My brave Black Bess stepped gallantly into the water, without a smidgen of hesitation.

The moon shone on the water and helped me see my way. When we reached the channel I wove my fingers tight in Bess's mane and hung on as she began to swim. Then I slid off her back, still holding on to her neck. I floated beside my gallant little mare, using my free arm to paddle along. The icy water soaked through my woolens and my teeth chattered. I couldn't think about the cold. We just had to cross the sound. Then I could change into the dry clothes tied about my shoulders.

Bess kept swimming. Stretching up her neck to keep her nose above water, she swam steadily toward the point. I felt her shivering, too.

"Poor Bess, what have I asked of you," I whispered.

If only I could sleep a little while. I shook my head violently. "No!" Giving up meant death to the horses, and if I slept, it would be an eternal sleep. I tightened my grip on my pony's mane.

Bess suddenly lurched forward, jerking my arm so it hurt. Then I felt the bottom. We had made it across the channel. The breeze blew an icy chill through my wet clothes. We were halfway. I pulled myself back onto Bess. "Please, let us make the shore before we freeze to death," I prayed again.

And we did reach the shore of Church Island, which was actually a point that jutted out into the sound. The cold had by then sunk into my very bones. I was shivering so hard I could hardly do my buttons as I changed into my somewhat-less-than-dry clothes. I pulled on the wool stockings and wiggled my toes. Slowly the feeling came back. Next, I put on the pair of leather boots. My fingers were so numb from cold I could hardly hold onto my boots to pull them up. They were wet, but the stockings were a barrier and for now would keep my feet dry enough.

Rubbing Bess's coat hard with the oilskin's rough side dried some of the wet from her coat and helped warm her. Bess quit shivering. After I finished drying her I chucked my wet clothes into the fork of a nearby tree. With my skirt tucked back between my legs, I remounted. I was so cold I worried that I might freeze to death before I could complete my mission, but I quickly dismissed the thought; I did not have time for melancholy.

I put Bess into a dead run. Once we found the Dismal Swamp trail, I had to trust my pony's animal instinct. Even with the trees bare, the woods were so thick the moonlight was naught. Briars tore at my clothes and branches caught me in the face, so that I had to bury my head in Bess's mane while I held on for dear life. Thoughts of Lord Dunmore's soldiers bearing down on our beautiful ponies made it possible to ignore the darkness and the cold. I remembered tales Grandpa used to tell me of panthers, wolves and the huge bears that lived in this swamp. The two things that gave me comfort were remembering Grandpa's tendency to exaggerate and my belief in prayer.

We had gone a few more miles through the forest when I heard a sound that made my blood run colder, if that was possible. It was a bloodcurdling scream. I thought, *There must be a woman being murdered or perhaps in the throes of childbirth.*

Regaining my wits, I knew the sound came from neither, but must be from a panther. Many times I'd heard Grandpa liken the cry of the big cat to a woman's scream.

I felt Bess's muscles quiver. "Just run, Bess, keep going, girl. We can outrun any ole cat! Run!" I could feel my poor pony's heart pounding and feared it might burst, but dared not slow her. The scream faded as Bess put distance between us and the cat. I offered another prayer, this time one of thanks.

Chapter Seventeen

Fear had turned my stomach quamish, which only added to the misery of the cold. The fear gave me all the more determination to reach Perquimans. The trail through the Dismal was treacherous for Bess. She stumbled on several occasions because of the mud and cypress knees that jutted up from the ground. Nevertheless, she was able to pull herself up each time and continued to run, toting my weight without complaint.

With great relief, I saw the moon's light reflecting on a group of rooftops; I was certain it was Camden up ahead. Reaching the edge of town, I whispered for Bess to walk. I didn't want to wake any well-meaning townspeople. They would surely want me to stop and explain why I was out riding this time of night. I pulled my sleeves down over my hands, which now ached from the cold. My toes were also getting cold again, the dampness of my boots having soaked through my stockings.

Once we passed through the small town I put Bess back into a gallop. It was only a few miles to Elizabeth City, then twenty or thirty to Hertford. I couldn't be sure, but the road would certainly be better than the trail through the swamp.

Entering Elizabeth City, I slowed my pony to a walk, hoping that at this late hour, the town crier would be dozing.

"Who goes there?" I heard someone shout, just as we reached the west side of town.

I didn't know whether to gallop away or answer, addled as I was by cold and fatigue.

"I say there, who goes!"

I decided to do both. Turning my head toward the crier, I hollered, "It is I, Betsy Dowdy! I am carrying news to General Skinner! Lord Dunmore is coming!"

Leaning forward over my pony's neck, I spoke right in her ear. "Go, girl!"

My beautiful, noble Bess ran like she was running for her life. Which she really was. If we didn't get to Skinner's camp in time, it could be the end of her and all of the Banker ponies.

I heard some shouting and a musket shot behind me.

"We can't give up now, girl," I whispered hoarsely. "We can't give up."

My throat was raw after screaming my reply. I felt feverish, and I ached through my joints from the cold. "Poor Bess," I said out loud. "She must be exhausted as well."

From the Diary of Rebecca Dowdy
December 6, 1775

No one can ever imagine my distress this morning when I found a note on Betsy's pillow telling me she was taking Bess and riding to Hertford to tell General Skinner about Lord Dunmore's advance on the Carolinas. That ride is over fifty miles. If I live to be a hundred, I will never understand what could have made her do such a thing.

Josiah says she is the bravest girl he has ever heard of, and he is proud of her, as I should be also. He said not to worry, Betsy knows that sound as well as anyone alive.

I know he was only trying to calm me. He was just as frantic as I when I screamed him awake this morning. His eyes do not lie. He dashed out into the dark to find

Sam. They launched the skiff at the break of dawn and started across the sound. By then it had begun to breeze up and the water was rough.

All I can think of is that I may lose my daughter and my husband both.

Not knowing what else to do, I made a pot of chamomile tea. I have been walking the floor the whole rest of the day, praying out loud for the safe return of my family. The water boiled out of the pot, and I never bothered to put on more. How can I sit still long enough to drink tea, anyway?

The sun rose this morning, turning the whole sky an angry red. "Red in the morning, sailors take warning."

Grandpa Dowdy, don't come with your ridiculous proverbs now. This is all your fault, filling a young girl's head full of tales of adventure.

She would never have even thought of taking off in the night had it not been for you!

Dear God, just bring my daughter and husband safely home. And forgive me my anger.

Chapter Eighteen

I saw their tents in the distance, tinged pink by the glow from the rising sun. Fog fingered its ghostly way through the camp, winding around the tents. I could see the red embers of their campfires and longed for the fire's warmth. By this time my fingers were numb, but I was so cold, my body shook all over. Just seeing the camp brought tears of relief streaming down my face.

"We did it, Bess. We're here!"

A flash of light and loud noise brought Bess to a sudden stop. I lurched to one side, nearly falling off. The bullet whizzed by us, only inches away, and hit the trunk of a nearby tree.

I tried to scream, "Don't shoot!" My voice sounded like a bullfrog's croak.

"Halt, who goes there?" a man shouted back.

I gathered all the strength I could muster to call back an answer. "It is Betsy Dowdy. I have come to bring news to General Skinner!"

By then the whole camp had stopped what they were doing and were looking at Bess and me. A sight we must have been, wet, cold and filthy.

"Come, girl. What is it? What are you talking about? Where have you come from?" The man helped me off Bess, but I nearly fell to the ground. My legs were too weak to support my weight.

"Someone get the doctor," he ordered.

"No," I said. "No, I must see General Skinner."

"Yes, ma'am. Go get the General," he barked. "And the doctor. Now! Just sit down, right here." He steered me toward a box near the fire.

"Bess, please, can someone see to Bess, my horse."

A soldier handed me a hot cup of coffee, which I accepted gratefully. Another man led Bess over to the picket line and began to rub her down with a rag.

I was shivering so hard I spilled the coffee, so the man held it to my lips while I sipped the strong, black liquid. The soldier who had given me the coffee brought me a blanket and wrapped it around my shoulders. I could hear murmuring as a small group started to form around me. I held my hands out to the warmth of their fire, but in a few moments the heat brought about a pain so severe I nearly came to tears.

Two men approached me. I guessed they were General Skinner and the doctor who had been summoned.

"This girl needs to be out of the weather, she is near frozen," he said as he laid the palm of his hand against my brow.

Then he examined my hands. "Frostbite," he said through clenched teeth.

"Ma'am, tell me where you have come from and why you are here." The general's voice was concerned.

"It's Lord Dunmore, sir. He has barricaded Great Bridge and taken Portsmouth and says Norfolk is next. From there he plans to sail down to the Carolinas. If you can take your men to meet Colonel Howe, you can stop Dunmore."

"How do you know this, girl? Where have you come from?"

"I come from Currituck Banks. Mr. Jarvis brought the news over today. He'd been to Church

Island, and someone showed it to him in the news-paper. And folks were there, folks who'd run away. Dunmore destroyed everything, burned houses, killed livestock, and horses. You've got to stop him! Mr. Jarvis says Dunmore will slaughter all our Banker horses and burn our houses, too."

I had no more than finished the last sentence when everything started spinning inside my head and I collapsed. Fortunately, the doctor caught me before I fell off the box.

I woke up in a fine feather bed, wrapped in a downy comforter, at the home of General Skinner. Lavinia Skinner, one of his three daughters, told me he and the militia were well on their way to Great Bridge.

"You were nearly frozen to death, and your fingers are frostbitten. The bandages have to stay on until the blistering heals, and you are to stay in bed. The doctor said so, before he left with my father." Lavinia sounded like a very capable nurse.

"Where is my Bess, I must go see to her." I tried to sit up, but my head started spinning again. I decided to do as Lavinia said and laid back into the soft goosedown bed.

"Now, just you don't worry about your mare," said Lavinia as she tucked the coverlet tightly about my shoulders. "Dolly has given her a nice hot mash and wisped her down good from head to tail. Dolly is quite daft when it comes to horses. If all were not well with your Bess, why she'd sleep right in the stable with her."

I must have still looked doubtful, because

Lavinia continued tucking and talking. "I never saw the like of Dolly. She can't stand to see any animal suffer. When she was just a little girl, not more than four or five, she found a baby bird fallen out of its nest. She nursed it night and day, feeding it mealy worms she found in the corncrib, and kept it warm by candlelight. The bird actually survived. So don't worry a bit over your Bess, she's in fine hands."

Lavinia gave me some soup that tasted good, but it nearly exhausted me to partake of it. I was soon back to sleep; not even the burning in my fingers could keep me awake. I slept for three days, only waking when Lavinia roused me to minister to my injuries and persuade me to sip more of her broth.

Chapter Nineteen

On the fourth morning, when I opened my eyes, Father was sitting in a chair next to my bed. I looked around the room, trying to focus on something familiar and shake the sense of confusion. A walnut dresser with a tall mirror hanging over it stood in the corner across the room. Where was the simple oak chest of drawers that Grandpa had built? The walls were painted a sunny yellow instead of the white I remembered. The breeze coming through the tall windows ruffled the green curtains, but I missed the smell of salt air. Nor could I hear the gulls laughing.

Slowly, things came into sharper focus, and I began to remember. I wasn't in my room, or my home at Chapel Field. No, I was in the home of

General William Skinner, being nursed by his daughter, Lavinia. All of the events that had led me to this place rushed back into my memory. I had no idea how long I'd been unconscious.

Father must have come after me when he found my note.

"Father, I am sorry. I know I shouldn't sneak off in the night, but I had to tell them about Lord Dunmore. I knew Mother would never let me go. And the air was breezing up, so I was afraid the skiff wouldn't make it in time, and what if Lord Dunmore were to come down the coast and burn our house and take our ponies? I couldn't let him do it, Father."

I looked at Father, but I couldn't tell what he was thinking. It seemed he was smiling, but trying hard not to let it show. He didn't speak for what seemed like a long, long time.

"That was a foolish thing you did, Betsy Dowdy." He was trying to sound stern, but then his voice caught, and I feared he was going to cry.

He swallowed hard and continued with his lecture. "Yes, and do you know what a risk you took? It is a miracle you are still alive. Your mother was in a terrible state when I left.

"There now. What is done is done," he said with a sigh. "Betsy, your warning came in time. Howe and Skinner's men defeated Dunmore in just thirty minutes! What's more, the rascal is out of Norfolk and retreating to sea. I don't think we'll be hearing any more from him. North Carolina, and your ponies, are safe."

From the Diary of Rebecca Dowdy
December 11, 1775

I couldn't decide whether to skin her alive or embrace her, so I just stood there in the hallway and cried when Josiah brought Betsy home. Her poor fingers were blistered and red from the frostbite and she was pale as could be.

"We did it, Mother, we beat old Dunmore. We and our ponies are safe," she said. Her voice was weak, barely above a whisper. Yet she insisted she had to see her precious ponies before I could put her to bed. I went with her, climbing over the dunes to the little hammock where the herd usually gathered.

"Look, Mother. Did you ever see anything so beautiful? I can't bear to imagine these islands without them." Betsy's eyes teared up and she sat

down in the sand. She pulled up her knees and wrapped her arms around her legs. She sat that way, gazing at the blacks, bays, and chestnuts that grazed and milled around lazily. "Don't you see, Mother? I had to do it."

There was nothing I could say to dispute her action or her words. Deep in my heart I was proud of her, and I saw why the wild ponies meant so much to Betsy. She shares with them the spirit of independence. Is there a better symbol of freedom than a horse grazing in the marsh or galloping in the surf? To ride as Betsy does, with such abandon of all weaknesses and fear, must be a wonderful thing.

Yes, I understood.

I walked with my daughter back to the house, fixed some hot chamomile tea, and tucked her into bed. Like it or not, it would be a few days before she regained strength enough to go back to her rambunctious ways.

Epilogue

Our fight for independence was a long and bloody one. Thousands of lives were lost. Although Bess and the ponies were unharmed, and we at Currituck Banks lived in comparative safety, North Carolina lost many good people in the War for Independence.

On July 2, 1776, delegates from twelve of the colonies passed a resolution drafted by Richard Henry Lee of Virginia, that "These United Colonies are, and of right ought to be, free and independent States." Two days later, the Second Continental Congress approved the Declaration of Independence.

It took seven more years before the United States and Great Britain signed the final peace treaty in Paris, France.

Mr. Isaac Druman courted me, we fell deeply in love, and were engaged to be married when he was called to arms. Soon afterward he was killed in the Battle of Moore's Creek.

I never cared to marry anyone after that. I stayed at Chapel Field in Grandpa's house, enjoying the freedom so valiantly won by our men and women.

Star grew into a beautiful stallion, easily winning his position as herd sire. He fathered a generation of sturdy Banker ponies, many of them sharing his speed and stamina as well as his shining black coat.

Black Bess gave me many more years of pleasure as we rode along the ocean shore, stirring up laughing gulls and sandpipers. I still delighted in letting my hair hang loose to fly in the wind while we galloped in the surf.

As my hair became streaked with gray and Bess's gaits began to falter, I satisfied myself by sitting among the sea oats atop Penny's Hill and watching my beautiful ponies while the setting sun splashed crimson and gold across the sky. There I watched Bess spend her last days peacefully grazing among the sand dunes of Currituck Banks.

Historical Notes

The story of Betsy Dowdy is an intriguing one. Of course whenever we hear of a legend we wonder about its origin. We wonder if it is true.

I researched whether Betsy's story was fact or fiction, and found some interesting information at the State Library and Archives of North Carolina in Raleigh. I learned that a Josiah and Rebecca Dowdy had lived on Currituck Banks in the 1700s and that they had a daughter named Betsy, among other children. I also found a book, *The Heritage of Currituck County*, compiled by The Albemarle Genealogical Society and published by Hunter Publishing Company, which convinced me of the story's validity.

From that book I learned that Richard B. Creecy, the great-grandson of Penelope Skinner

Creecy, first published Betsy's story. Penelope was one of General William Skinner's daughters. She handed the story down to her children, her grand-children and her great-grandson, Mr. Creecy.

Richard Creecy was the editor of *The Economist*, an Elizabeth City newspaper. In 1901, he published the story of Betsy and her pony, Black Bess, in his book, *Grandfather's Tales*.

While my story is based on these few facts, its details are entirely products of my imagination. You will find references to events that really took place and some that maybe took place and others that only existed in my mind, until I put them on paper.

Bibliography

Ashe, Samuel A'Court. *History of North Carolina, Volume I 1584-1783.* Greensboro, NC: Charles L. Van Noppen, 1925.

Barefoot, Daniel W. *Touring the Backroads of North Carolina's Upper Coast.* Winston-Salem, NC: John F. Blair, 1995.

Dowdy, Margaret. "Grandfather's Tales: Richard B. Creecy 1901." In *Heritage of Currituck County,* edited by Jo Anna Heath. Winston-Salem, NC: Hunter Publishing Co., 1985.

"The Ride of Betsy Dowdy." *Kids' Connection Dare County's Outer Banks,* pg. 5. Dare County Tourist Bureau.

Samuelson, Nancy B. "Revolutionary War Women and the Second Oldest Profession." *Minerva Quarterly Report*, vol. 7, no. 2 (Summer 1989): 16-25.

Sealy, Mabel Ivey. "Betsy Dowdy's Ride." Excerpted from *Betsy Dowdy's Ride*, by Nell Wise Wechter. Winston Salem, NC: John F. Blair, 1960. Reprinted in *Dateline: Currituck County*, vol. #6 (Fall 1997): 8.

Watson, Alan D. *Perquimans County, A Brief History*. Raleigh, NC: NC Division of Archives & History, 1987.

Wechter, Nell Wise. *Betsy Dowdy's Ride*. Winston-Salem, NC: John F. Blair, 1960.

Wolfram, Walt & Natalie Schilling-Estes. *Hoi Toide on the Outer Banks.* Chapel Hill, NC: UNC Press, 1997.

Teacher's Guide

Dates to Remember

1765 – On March 22, British Parliament passed the Stamp Act. It took effect on November 1st. With the passage of the Stamp Act, the British imposed a tax on almost any kind of printed materials, including newspapers, legal documents, and even playing cards. It was the first direct tax on the American colonies' goods.

March 5, 1770 – Boston Massacre. A crowd of colonists was throwing snowballs at British guards, a riot started, and the British fired on the crowd.

November 20, 1772 – Samuel Adams organized the Committee of Correspondence to let people know that the British were violating the rights of the colonists.

1773 – The British Parliament passed the Tea Act. On December 16, 1773, the Boston Tea Party took place.

March 1774 – British Parliament enacted the Intolerable Acts, closing Boston Harbor to commerce in retaliation for the Boston Tea Party.

September 5, 1774 – The First Continental Congress met in Philadelphia, Pennsylvania to defend American rights.

October 25, 1774 – Organized by Penelope Barker, a group of women in Edenton, North Carolina met and drew up a proclamation. They resolved not to drink tea imported from India by the British, nor to purchase any more imported fashions until the Stamp Act was repealed.

March 30, 1775 – The New England Restraining Act was passed against Massachusetts's Bay, New Hampshire, Rhode Island, and Connecticut. This act restrained commercial fishing and foreign trade, except with Britain, with force if needed.

April 18, 1775 – Paul Revere made his famous ride from Boston to Lexington, warning colonists that "The British are coming!"

April 19, 1775 – British troops were ordered to destroy military supplies that the Patriots had stored at Concord. The first battle of the American Revolutionary War—the Battle of Lexington and Concord—was fought in Massachusetts.

August 23, 1775 – King George III issued a proclamation officially declaring the thirteen colonies to be in a state of rebellion, and ordering the rebellion suppressed.

November 1775 – Lord Dunmore issued a proclamation declaring martial law in Virginia. He captured Portsmouth, and bragged that Norfolk was defenseless. On November 31, 1775, the *Virginia Gazette* reported that Lord Dunmore wrote, "I really believe we should reduce this colony to a proper sense of their duty." In the same paper George Washington was reported to have said that Dunmore needed to be crushed and that the fate of the colonies depended on getting him out of Norfolk.

December 9, 1775 – Dunmore was defeated in Virginia's Battle of Great Bridge. Three weeks later, Norfolk was captured by the "rebels."

January 1, 1776 – Norfolk was burned and British rule was ended in Virginia.

February 27, 1776 – The Patriots defeated the Loyalists at Moore's Creek, North Carolina.

April 12, 1776 – North Carolina's Provincial Congress was the first to empower its delegates in the Continental Congress to vote for independence from Britain.

July 4, 1776 – The Declaration of Independence was signed.

September 3, 1783 – The Treaty of Paris was signed by Britain, Spain, the Netherlands, France, and America. The Revolutionary War officially ended.

Activities

1. Write a monologue pretending you are one of the famous characters mentioned in the book– Blackbeard, Penelope Barker, Lord Dunmore, George Washington. Dress in costume and perform the monologue.

2. Have an Edenton-style tea party. Menu – herbal tea (with milk and honey), scones, strawberry jam, pecan cookies, and roasted peanuts. Discuss the reasons for boycotting tea and other products imported from England.

3. Learn what kind of dances the colonial people danced at a ball, learn to do one and "have a ball!" One favorite colonial dance was the minuet. (Ask your school's dance teacher to help.)

4. Make a model of Betsy's house. Remember it had a large porch, tall windows, and the kitchen was a separate building. What materials did Betsy's grandfather use to build the house? Are houses still built like that on the Outer Banks?

5. Make an illustrated/relief map of Betsy's ride.

6. Bring a food item that is mentioned in the book to school.

7. Have an oyster roast. Buy oysters in the shell from a seafood market. Wash the shells with clean water to remove sand and mud. Put them into a large pot with about two inches of water in the bottom. Heat until the water boils and produces steam to cook the oysters. They are done when the shells open. You can also plan a class trip to an oyster bar to taste steamed oysters.

Questions

1. In Chapter One, where did Betsy say her Grandpa lived before coming to North Carolina? How did he make a living?

If you know where your ancestors lived before coming to America, share this with the class.

2. Why wasn't Betsy worried about the events taking place in the colonies and Britain?

Discuss whether you think that many people wait until something affects them in a personal way before they really become concerned.

3. Why were the kitchens of colonial houses built separately from the main houses?

4. In colonial times, how did people keep cool during hot weather?

5. Discuss how Betsy's lifestyle was different from the lifestyle of her cousin, Johnny.

6. How did the wild horses get to Currituck Banks?

7. What caused Betsy to ride Bess to General Skinner's camp?

8. Why did Rebecca Dowdy worry about Betsy's un-ladylike behavior?

9. Why didn't Betsy's family own slaves?

10. What little creatures did Betsy sometimes find in oyster shells that she liked to eat—legs and all?

Answers

1. He was from Ireland and was captain of a whaling ship.

2. The events seemed far away and the people living on the Outer Banks were self-sufficient, so they did not affect her personally. At that time North Carolina was still mostly a wilderness except for a few port cities like Edenton, New Bern and Wilmington. People did not depend on imported goods, but grew their own food and made most of their clothes.

3. In the event that the kitchen caught fire, the whole house wasn't likely to burn down. Also, it kept the heat from cooking out of the rest of the house. Remember, there were no air-conditioners or fire departments in those days.

4. Houses were built with tall windows to let in the breeze. Ladies used handheld fans. Houses also had large porches, which were places to socialize or do sit-down chores while taking advantage of the shade and breeze.

5. Betsy's family made their living fishing. Johnny's family owned a plantation. Johnny's family owned slaves and Betsy's did not. Betsy lived on an isolated island and Johnny lived on the mainland near a large town. There were not as many formal social events on the islands as there were in Edenton where Johnny lived.

6. They were descended from horses brought to the coast of North Carolina by Spanish explorers in the 1500s.

7. Lord Dunmore's attack on Norfolk and his plan to invade North Carolina. She was afraid he'd kill the wild horses that lived near her home.

8. She was afraid Betsy might get hurt on one of her escapades. She also worried Betsy might not find a good husband if she didn't learn how to act more like a lady.

9. They were Quakers and opposed slavery for religious reasons.

10. Tiny crabs.

Classroom Resources

Find out more about colonial America, North Carolina's wild horses, and historic northeastern North Carolina:

Museums and Tours:

Historic Edenton Tours
PO Box 474
108 North Broad St., Edenton, NC 27932
phone 252-482-2637

Museum of the Albemarle
1116 US Hwy 17 South
Elizabeth City, NC 27909-9806
www.albemarle-nc.com/MOA
phone 252-335-1453

On the Internet:

The History Net—Where History Lives on the Web. This site contains lots of useful historical information on a variety of topics. For specific information on American history, visit:
www.americanhistory.about.com

18th Century—Relive History. The Live 18th Century Homepage has lots of good links about colonial history:
www.members.aol.com/liv18thc

NC Horse News. This site features an article about North Carolina's wild horse population:
www.nchorsenews.com/stories.htm

Outer Banks Explorer.com—Wild Ponies (with photographs):
www.outerbanksexplorer.com/infopages/ponies.htm

Corolla Wild Horse Fund. This website gives the history of the Corolla herd:
www.corollawildhorses.com

History of Edenton, North Carolina:
www.edenton.com/history

Archiving Early America. This website features historic documents from the 1700s:
www.earlyamerica.com

Vocabulary

Chapter One

Cloak – A sleeveless outer garment, worn around the shoulders and fastened at the neck.

Mainland – The continent, or large mass of land. A mainlander is a person who does not live on the islands, but on the mainland.

Nor'easter – A storm caused by strong winds from the north and the east.

Skiff – A small flat-bottomed boat with a pointed bow, usually rowed, but sometimes fitted with a sail.

Withers – The point where a horse's neck is joined to the shoulder, the highest part of the back.

Diary Entry, Nov. 28, 1774

Chastise – To scold or punish.

Chapter Two

Aristocratic – Upper-class.

Banker pony or horse – A breed of ponies native to the Outer Banks. They are descendants of Spanish horses brought to the New World by early explorers.

Chores – Regular household duties.

Collard greens – A leafy green vegetable that grows well in North Carolina and other southern states.

Fodder beans – Green beans that have been strung and hung up to dry. Native Americans and early settlers used this method to preserve them for the winter.

Hindquarters – The rear end.

Inlet – An opening through two landmasses through which water flows.

Planter – A rich farmer or plantation owner.

Quaker – A Christian religious denomination built around peaceful ideas and principles.

Sound – A body of water formed by the widening of a river before it empties into the ocean.

Succulent – Juicy.

Waft – To rush or move through the air or water.

Chapter Three

Daft – Silly or crazy.

Osnabrig – A coarse, unbleached fabric woven of linen and cotton, sometimes hemp. It was first made in Osnabruck, Germany. During colonial times it was also made in Lancashire, England and Scotland.

Salvage – Property saved from a disaster, such as a shipwreck.

Stamp Act – See Dates to Remember.

Chapter Four

Britches – Also known as breeches, these are short pants that reach to the knees.

Meehonkey – A hide-and-seek game.

Skeeters – A special pronunciation for mosquitoes, commonly used on the Outer Banks of North Carolina and in the South.

Diary Entry, Nov. 29, 1774

Melancholy – Sad or depressed.

Militia – Soldiers who were private citizens, called on in emergency situations.

Chapter Seven

Bankers – People who live on the Outer Banks.

Islanders – People who live on an island.

Chapter Eight

Equestrian – A person who rides horses.

Hull – The body of a ship or boat.

Seamstress – A woman who sews.

Tedious – Slow and tiresome.

Chapter Nine

Bodice – The top part of a woman's dress. The bodice was sleeveless and held together in the front with laces or buttons. It was separate from the skirt.

Boycott – To join with others and agree not to buy, use or do business with someone as a way to protest the actions of that person or to get them to change.

Curtsy – A gesture of respect made by slightly lowering the body while bending the knees.

Petticoat – An underskirt, or slip.

Twice-made – Made over.

Chapter Ten

Canter – A fast, three-beat gait.

Caplet – A short cloak.

Hacking – Casual horseback riding

Jubilant – Happy and joyful.

Luminous – Bright, giving out light.

Chapter Eleven

Breeding stock – Animals kept for the purpose of producing offspring, usually of superior quality.

Corpse – A dead body.

Chapter Twelve

Redcoats – British soldiers, so named because the coats of their uniforms were red.

Chapter Thirteen

Colt – A young male horse. A young female horse is called a filly.

Foal – A baby horse.

Diary Entry, Nov. 28, 1775

Coiffeur – Hairdo, usually refering to a dressy hair arrangement.

Chapter Fourteen

Blowfish – Also called puffer fish, these are fish found in the Atlantic that swell up when they are frightened. Some species are covered with spines. They are poisonous to eat.

Cordage – Cord, string.

Weanling – A young horse that is no longer nursing.

Yarns – Stories, tall tales.

Chapter Sixteen

Airish – Cool and windy weather conditions.

Panther – A large wildcat, also called a cougar.

Shift – A woman's loose-fitting, sleeved undergarment, resembling a long shirt. It was also worn as a nightshirt.

Chapter Seventeen

Crier – A person who "cries out" announcements or warnings to the community.

Quamish – Having an upset stomach.

Diary Entry, Dec. 6, 1775

Chamomile tea – An herbal tea that is soothing to the nerves, made from the chamomile plant.

Chapter Eighteen

Frostbite – A condition caused by exposure to freezing temperatures in which body tissue is damaged.

Dates to Remember

British Parliament – The law-making body of England, made up of two parts: the House of Commons and the House of Lords.

Loyalists – Colonists loyal to the British cause. The Patriots also referred to them as Tories.

Patriots – Colonial revolutionists rebelling against British rule and seeking independence for the colonies.

Epilogue

Battle of Moore's Creek – Took place on February 27, 1776. The Patriots won, driving out the Loyalists and securing Moore's Creek Bridge near Wilmington, North Carolina.

Continental Congress – Made up of representatives from the colonies, this group first met in Philadelphia in 1774.

About the Author

For most of her life, Donna Campbell Smith has lived only a short distance from North Carolina's Outer Banks. It's only natural that she chose these barrier islands as the setting for her young adult historical novels, *An Independent Spirit* and *Pale as the Moon*. Donna is a certified riding instructor with an AAS degree in equine technology and has been a Master North Carolina 4-H Horse Program volunteer for over twenty years. Her articles and essays have appeared in several print and online magazines, including *USA Equestrian, Horse Show, Young Rider, Boys' Life, Our State, Carolina Country, NC Horse News.com, Stablegate.com* and various small press magazines.